Michael Underwood and The Murder Room

〉〉〉 This title is part of The Murder Room, our series dedicated to making available out-of-print or hard-to-find titles by classic crime writers.

Crime fiction has always held up a mirror to society. The Victorians were fascinated by sensational murder and the emerging science of detection; now we are obsessed with the forensic detail of violent death. And no other genre has so captivated and enthralled readers.

Vast troves of classic crime writing have for a long time been unavailable to all but the most dedicated frequenters of second-hand bookshops. The advent of digital publishing means that we are now able to bring you the backlists of a huge range of titles by classic and contemporary crime writers, some of which have been out of print for decades.

From the genteel amateur private eyes of the Golden Age and the femmes fatales of pulp fiction, to the morally ambiguous hard-boiled detectives of mid twentieth-century America and their descendants who walk our twenty-first century streets, The Murder Room has it all. **〉〉〉**

The Murder Room
Where Criminal Minds Meet

themurderroom.com

Michael Underwood (1916–1992)

Michael Underwood (the pseudonym of John Michael Evelyn) was born in Worthing, Sussex and educated at Christ Church College, Oxford. He was called to the Bar in 1939 and served in the British army during World War Two. He returned to work in the Department of Public Prosecutions until his retirement in 1976, and wrote almost 50 crime novels informed by his career in the law. His five series characters include Sergeant Nick Atwell and lawyer Rosa Epton, of whom is was said by the *Washington Post* that she 'outdoes Perry Mason'.

By Michael Underwood

Simon Manton

Murder on Trial (1954)
Murder Made Absolute (1955)
Death on Remand (1956)
False Witness (1957)
Lawful Pursuit (1958)
Arm of the Law (1959)
Cause of Death (1960)
Death by Misadventure (1960)
Adam's Case (1961)
The Case Against Philip
   Quest (1962)
Girl Found Dead (1963)
The Crime of Colin Wise (1964)
The Anxious Conspirator (1956)

Richard Monk

The Man Who Died on
   Friday (1967)
The Man Who Killed Too
   Soon (1968)

Martin Ainsworth

The Shadow Game (1970)
Trout in the Milk (1971)
Reward for a Defector (1973)
The Unprofessional Spy (1975)

Rosa Epton

A Pinch of Snuff (1974)
Crime upon Crime (1980)
Double Jeopardy (1981)

Goddess of Death (1982)
A Party to Murder (1983)
Death in Camera (1984)
The Hidden Man (1985)
Death at Deepwood
   Grange (1986)
The Injudicious Judge (1982)
The Uninvited Corpse (1987)
Dual Enigma (1988)
A Compelling Case (1989)
A Dangerous Business (1990)
Rosa's Dilemma (1990)
The Seeds of Murder (1991)
Guilty Conscience (1992)

Nick Atwell

The Juror (1975)
Menaces, Menaces (1976)
The Fatal Trip (1977)
Murder with Malice (1977)
Crooked Wood (1978)

Standalone titles

A Crime Apart (1966)
Shem's Demise (1970)
The Silent Liars (1970)
Anything but the Truth (1978)
Smooth Justice (1979)
Victim of Circumstance (1979)
A Clear Case of Suicide (1980)
Hand of Fate (1981)

Murder with Malice

Michael Underwood

An Orion book

Copyright © Isobel Mackenzie 1977

The right of Michael Underwood to be identified as the author of this work has been asserted in accordance with the Copyright, Designs and Patents Act 1988.

This edition published by
The Orion Publishing Group Ltd
Orion House
5 Upper St Martin's Lane
London WC2H 9EA

An Hachette UK company
A CIP catalogue record for this book is available from the British Library

ISBN 978 1 4719 0802 6

www.orionbooks.co.uk

Chapter 1

Suspended! The word raced round Nick Attwell's head with the throbbing persistence of a madly barking dog. It pushed every other thought aside. It was as though the word had infiltrated his skull and multiplied itself a million times until his whole head rang with it.

"The Deputy Commissioner has therefore decided, Sergeant Attwell, that you should be suspended from duty pending investigation of the complaint which has been made against you."

Thus had spoken the Commander of C.O.C.I. in a stiff, uncomfortable tone. Then because he was a kindly man and had disliked being the bearer of such harsh news to a young officer of whom he had always heard well, he had added in a gentler tone, "Don't despair, Attwell, nobody's saying you're guilty of anything just because it's Sir Guy Frensham who's made the complaint. But as you know, the Commissioner is obliged to have it investigated by A.10 and it's better all round that you should be suspended pending the outcome. We have to avoid any possible embarrassment to the Commissioner. . . ." His voice had trailed away, but Nick knew well enough what he meant. When someone like Sir Guy Frensham, who was an ex-M.P. and a current

1

T.V. pundit, made a complaint against a police officer, everyone reacted nervously. The investigation procedure must not only move swiftly into action, but must be seen to do so with impartial zeal.

"Hey, why don't you look where you're going, mate, you nearly had me off!"

The tone was sufficiently sharp to impinge upon Nick's tumultuous thoughts. He stepped quickly back on to the pavement as a young man on a moped straightened out from a potentially disastrous wobble and accelerated away like an angry mosquito.

More by good fortune than judgment, Nick reached the farther curb and walked away from the huge building which loomed behind him. Until a quarter of an hour before, it had been a largely friendly if faintly impersonal building, the working-place of all those police officers and civilians who comprised Scotland Yard.

But for Nick, there was nothing friendly about it now. It had become cold and hostile. He could feel its hostility at his back as he quickened his pace to get away from it. He had no clear idea where he was going; his only object was to put distance between himself and the building out of which he had just walked in numbed disbelief. Suspended!

He would have found it difficult to say what made him cross the road and enter Westminster Abbey. Although he could see it from his office window and passed by it several times a week, it was many years since he had been inside. Perhaps it was its very familiarity; perhaps, more, its open West door with its invitation to those seeking an answer to their problems.

The only times Nick went to church were weddings and christenings and the occasional funeral. And though he was wont to send up a prayer at moments of stress, it was always when he was walking along the street or standing in a bus queue. He hadn't been down on his knees to pray since he had left childhood. It seemed hypocritical to do so now and accordingly he just sat on a chair a few rows from the back and stared ahead of him. Despite the constant murmurings and movement of visitors, it was cool and soothing to sit there and to feel the drumming in his head begin to subside.

His attention had been drawn, when he first sat down, to a girl two rows in front of him and to his left. What had attracted his notice was her upright position of kneeling. Not resting her behind against the edge of the seat, her elbows were on the top of the chair in front and her face was covered by her hands. She was absolutely still and Nick wondered what she was praying about. For her, the posture was obviously as normal as it was unaccustomed for him, but somehow she helped to contribute to the timeless serenity of the great church.

He was staring up at one of the sweeping arches wondering just how he was going to break the news of his suspension to Clare when he heard a sudden gasp.

He looked toward the girl, who, though still kneeling, had turned and was staring straight at him with an expression of considerable suspicion. In the second before she spoke, he realised that she was as attractive as her long auburn hair had promised.

"My purse!" she said, still staring hard at Nick. "Someone's taken my purse."

He slid quickly from his seat and into the row between them.

"It was on the seat next to me," she said, indicating the chair to her left. "You must have seen who took it?"

Nick shook his head. "I'm afraid not. I wasn't looking that way and there are so many people moving up and down. It could have been anyone." This was especially true as the seat in question was the end one in the row. "You didn't hear anything?" he asked.

"No. It wasn't until I glanced round that I saw it had gone. What ought I to do?"

"Report it to the police."

"What good will that do?"

"Probably none, but you still ought to. The person may be arrested for something else and your purse could come to light."

"But not its contents," she remarked with a small twisted smile.

"What was in it?"

"A handkerchief, and about a couple of pounds."

"You certainly won't see the money again and the purse will probably end up in a litter basket. But at least it could have been worse."

"Oh, I never carry much money about with me in London. It's too risky with all your pickpockets and bag-snatchers around." Nick detected a note of reproach in the use of the word "your", but was really stung when she went on, "And the police seem quite helpless if not worse."

"That's certainly not true," he said vigorously.

She opened her eyes a fraction wider and stared at him for a second or two before speaking.

"Are you connected with them in some way?" she enquired with a quizzical smile.

"As a matter of fact I am."

"Oh, well, then I've reported the theft to the right person." She raised herself off her knees and sat down. "Do you want my particulars?"

"I'll show you the way to Rockmere Row Police Station. That's the place to report it."

The girl shrugged and, stepping past Nick, made for the door. He hurried after her. As they got outside, he said, "I'm sorry, I didn't mean to sound unhelpful, but I'm stationed at Scotland Yard and this is a matter for the local police. And, anyway. . . ."

The girl paused and searched his face—as though looking for the answer to the question she was about to ask. "What were you doing in Westminster Abbey in the middle of the afternoon? Were you on some secret mission or something?"

"No, nothing like that." It seemed to the girl as she waited for him to go on that he had gone into a trance. At last he re-focused his gaze on her and said, "What about a cup of tea?"

"Make it coffee and I'll come."

Her name was Alice Macpherson, she was 23 years old and she came from New Zealand. She had been in England for nine months and was currently working as an au pair with a family in North London. This was her regular afternoon off and she told Nick that she often dropped into a church to say her prayers. She was planning to return home in three months time after a winter sports holiday in Austria.

By the time Nick had learnt all this, she, for her part, knew that he was a Detective Sergeant in the Metropolitan Police, that he had a wife called Clare who was an ex-police officer and a ten month old baby son named Simon—and that he lived in a small house off Barnes Common. She also knew that he had recently passed his inspector's exam.

"So why aren't you an inspector now?" she asked, giving her coffee a further stir.

"One has to wait for a vacancy," he said in a tone of abrupt dejection.

"How long is that likely to be?" Alice asked, not understanding his sudden change of mood.

"Any old time. Possibly never in my case!" Instinct told her that she was on the verge of finding out why he had been sitting in the Abbey that afternoon. "I've been suspended from duty, I may be dismissed," he blurted out.

4

"What are you supposed to have done?" she asked quietly after a pause.

"Do you really want to know?"

"I wouldn't have asked if I didn't." She had the tact not to add, "and you wouldn't have brought me to this café and mentioned the subject if you didn't want to talk to someone about it." And, as she knew, a sympathetic stranger is often the best audience for the sort of unburdening which was about to come.

"I've been on a murder enquiry," he said, staring at a crumb on the table. "An old lady called Florence Isaacs was found murdered in her bedroom. She was a widow and lived alone in a large house up at Highgate. She had quite a lot of valuables and robbery was almost certainly the motive. She used to keep quite large amounts of loose cash around the house. In vases and between books and that sort of thing. There were signs that someone had been looking for money and jewelry which would indicate somebody with knowledge of her habits." He paused and flicked the crumb which had been holding his gaze off the table. "Suspicion fell on a couple of people. One was a young man named Unsworth who occupied a flat at the top of the house until a short time ago when she gave him the boot following a big row between them. There's evidence that Unsworth bore her a considerable grudge."

"What was the row over?"

"We don't know. Unsworth has disappeared and we've not yet been able to trace him. We only heard about the row from the daily woman and she couldn't tell us the details. Just said there'd been a row and that Mrs. Isaacs had refused to discuss it with anyone."

"You said two suspects," Alice prompted in the pause that followed.

"Yes, the other's a seventeen year old youth named Paul Frensham. He's the son of Sir Guy Frensham. Heard of *him*?"

Alice nodded, but Nick failed to observe her expression of quickening interest.

"Paul Frensham used to do odd gardening jobs for Mrs. Isaacs to earn a bit of pocket money. He was working there the afternoon she died. By all accounts he's a feckless young man and was always on the borrow. We hauled him in for questioning, but he denied all knowledge of the murder. But we found a freshly washed sweater he'd been wearing on the afternoon in question which he was evasive about, and he was generally unimpressive under interrogation. However, we didn't have enough to charge him and so he was allowed to go." Nick ran a finger along the edge of the table. His story had come out in staccato bursts which had left him seemingly breathless. As though he had been urgently dictating only the vitals of the case. "And now he's made this allegation through his father," he said in a taut voice. "It's utterly base, of course, and I suppose I shouldn't be surprised that a spoilt brat like Paul Frensham should make malicious attacks on the police. God knows, we're always vulnerable to false accusations, but that doesn't make it any better when you happen to be the target yourself; nor when it's someone like Sir Guy Frensham weighing in against you." He paused and added bitterly, "I wouldn't put it past him to try and whip up public support next time he's on T.V. I always did regard him as a phoney and now I know he's a dishonest one into the bargain."

"What exactly are you accused of?" Alice asked quietly in the pause that followed.

"Paul Frensham told his father that I'd asked him for £2000 in order to suppress a vital piece of evidence against him."

"What was the piece of evidence supposed to be?"

Nick made a mirthless sound. "It appears I didn't reveal that. Simply that I'd frame him if he didn't pay me the money."

"Why should he have picked on you?" Alice asked in a puzzled tone.

"Because I was the officer who went to his house and brought him to the Station for questioning. There's the further allegation that I browbeat him into letting me search his room. The way the complaint's been laid, he's made to sound a defenceless young schoolboy instead of a seventeen year old drop-out which is nearer the mark. If his father wants to make a public issue of it on television, I hope he'll disclose that his nasty young son was convicted in the Juvenile Court two years ago of assaulting another youth. Waited till the other boy's back was turned, then hit him over the head with a lump of wood just to clinch the argument they'd been having. That tells you the sort of person he is."

But Alice didn't seem to be listening. She was worrying one end of her lower lip with two white even teeth. Her expression was deeply thoughtful. Finally, she seemed to reach a decision and looked up.

"I've met Paul Frensham once," she said. Before Nick could speak, she went on, "It was about a couple of months ago at a disco in Hampstead. A girl in our party knew Kerstin. She's the Frenshams' Swedish au pair and she was there with Paul Frensham." She smiled apologetically. "I'm afraid that's all there really is. Kerstin and Paul joined us for a few minutes and soon afterwards they left."

Nick gave a sigh. It was as though a suddenly struck match had flickered out. But some comment seemed to be called for.

"Did you form any impression of him?"

"I thought he was quite good-looking in a rather young way. It was fairly clear that he didn't want to linger at our table. I heard afterwards from the girl who knew them that he was besotted with Kerstin, and spent all the time he could in her bed."

"Kerstin was out with the younger children when I went to the house; what sort of girl is she?"

"Very attractive if you go for the statuesque nordic type. She has lovely features and a rather grave air. In appearance cold and aloof you might say."

"But not cold all the way through?"

Alice smiled. "Not according to what I was told."

"How old is she?"

"About my age. Perhaps a year younger."

"But older than Paul?"

"Yes, by several years." She glanced at her watch. "I shall have to go in a few minutes. Do you really think I should report the theft of my purse? From what you say, there's little hope of my ever getting it back and it does seem rather a waste of time."

"As a policeman, I'm bound to say you ought to, but I'd understand if you didn't. I'm thankful there wasn't more than £2 in it."

"So am I!"

"You know, when I first saw you staring at me, I thought you believed that I'd taken it."

"Well, it did cross my mind. After all, you were closer to me than anyone else. But when you came springing forward, I knew it couldn't have been you." She pushed her chair back. "I've had a number of curious experiences in London, but this has been one of the oddest."

"I can't begin to tell you how grateful I am," Nick said earnestly. "But for you, I'd probably be in the river by now."

"I'm glad I saved you from that," she said, with a laugh. She paused in the act of standing up. "It's none of my business, but I'm just curious. Are you going to find it difficult explaining all this to your wife?"

"About meeting you?"

"No! About being suspended?"

"Less now than I'd thought. Talking to you has helped. And having been in the force herself means that she's aware of the things that can happen."

Alice held out her hand. "I hope everything works out all right for you. I'll certainly follow the case in the paper. The murder case, that is. If it was Paul Frensham who killed the old lady, I'll have added to life's experiences by meeting a murderer."

"You haven't given me your address," Nick said hastily as she turned to go. She glanced back with a quizzical expression. "And I've not given you mine. I mean, if you did learn anything further about Paul Frensham, I'd be very grateful if you'd call me. And it's not impossible that I might want to get in touch with you about some detail or other." Tearing a page from the back of his pocket-book, he divided it into two and gave her half to write down her address. "That's my home number," he said, handing her his half. With a grim little smile, he added, "I'll probably be in most of the day for the next few weeks."

Clare was half way down the stairs when she heard the key in the front door.

"Darling, how lovely, you're back early," she cried as the door opened and Nick came in.

Even in the second before she ran forward to kiss him, she realised that something had happened. His smile seemed to belong to a waxwork. And when they did kiss, it wasn't just that his breath smelt freshly of whisky, but as though someone other than the Nick she knew had taken possession of his body.

She stepped back and looked at him anxiously.

"Something's happened," she said. It came more as a statement than as a question. "What is it, Nick?"

"I've been suspended."

For a second or two she was silent, then determined to conceal the feeling of utter dismay the news had caused her, she ran forward and kissed him again.

"First a drink and then tell me."

He followed her into the kitchen and watched her fetch a can of lager from the refrigerator. She poured it out and handed it to him and then poured herself a glass of sherry.

They took their drinks into the living-room and sat down. Once Nick began, the whole story came out without any prompting from Clare. The only interruption came when Simon started crying upstairs. Clare looked hopefully toward her husband, but he shook his head.

"You go," he murmured stiffly. It was as though, she reflected sadly, he feared that a ten-months old baby might start asking him awkward questions. When she returned downstairs, he carried on exactly from where he had left off.

When he reached the end, he lay back in his chair with an air of exhaustion.

"I would hope," he said in a brittle sort of voice, "that people needn't get to know. I mean, is there any need for our respective parents to be told?"

"I know how you feel, darling, but I think it'll probably be best not to try and pretend anything. I'm not proposing we should broadcast the news up and down the street, but I think we should tell our parents and Bob and Sheila next door and take the sting out of it by saying that officers are frequently suspended while complaints are investigated, that in your case the complaint is completely unfounded and that your vindication and reinstatement is only a matter of time."

"You believe that?" he asked in a slightly hollow voice.

"Confidently."

"I hope you're right."

"Well, you didn't solicit a bribe from Paul Frensham, did you?" Clare asked in a tone of faint exasperation.

"Of course I didn't."

"Then he's lying and it's only a matter of time before he's shown to be lying. Just because he's the son of Sir Guy Frensham doesn't mean his word is going to be accepted at face value. Rather the reverse, one hopes. Nobody in their right mind would buy a second-hand television set on his father's say so."

"Nevertheless, I've let you and Simon and everyone else down."

"Don't be daft, darling. Having baseless complaints made against you is an occupational hazard in the police. You haven't let anybody down, least of all Simon who'd still love you if you were Jack the Ripper reincarnated."

Though she spoke robustly and had no doubts about her husband's innocence, Clare realised the strains to which his suspension from duty would inevitably give rise. She'd seen it happen during her own service. And it was always the genuinely innocent ones who were most affected. Well, it would be up to her to anticipate the strains and get him through the darker periods that lay ahead. As far as she was concerned, their two years of marriage had been the happiest of her life. She was deeply in love with her husband and had every reason to believe that he felt the same way about her. And having been in the police herself, the support she could now offer him might even be of a practical kind. She was already toying with the possibility of getting in touch with this Alice Macpherson. She was intrigued to find out just what sort of a girl it was who'd had this cathartic effect on her husband. And in Westminster Abbey of all places! But more than that she'd like to talk to her about Paul Frensham and his Swedish girlfriend.

The one thing that stuck out a mile to Clare was that Paul Frensham hadn't accused Nick just for sport. He must have done so with a strong motive. Could it have been that his motive was to get Nick taken off the case? If so, he had been successful. But why should he have wanted that? It was a question Clare couldn't answer at the moment, but it was one which was still knocking at her mind some hours later as she and Nick lay curled together in bed that night.

Chapter 2

Detective Chief Inspector Pitcher found himself in charge of the Isaacs murder investigation when various officers of superior rank fell by the wayside. He welcomed the chance of proving that his rapid promotion had not been due to anything other than merit, as whispers put out by one or two disgruntled colleagues had suggested.

"Peter Pitcher," one had sneered. "They'll be promoting Simple Simon next."

Still in his early thirties, Pitcher resembled a middle-grade young advertising executive more than a detective. He had a naturally neat appearance and kept up with fashion, at the same time avoiding the label "trendy".

He had a nice, if dull, wife who adored him and two children whom he adored.

At this moment he was sitting on the edge of a sofa leaning forward as though ready to spring and observing gravely the man who sat opposite him.

Oliver Gill was Mrs. Isaacs nephew and the room in which the two men were sitting was the drawing-room of Mrs. Isaacs house at 14 Teeling Road, N.2.

11

It was a large Victorian house in an overgrown garden of shrubs and it was surrounded by other houses of the same period. But whereas many of its neighbors had been converted into flats, number 14 was still one house, apart from the top floor which had been semi-converted to the extent of the installation of a kitchen and bathroom, though without a separate entrance from the outside.

On a low table between the two men rested an old fashioned jewelry box, its lid open.

"So the position is, Mr. Gill, that you can't really help me as to whether any of your aunt's jewelry is missing?"

"I'm afraid not, inspector. I've never actually seen the inside of the box before. I used to see her wearing various bits, but I'd no idea what she had." He peered into the box. "Have you any idea of its value?"

Pitcher shook his head. "Not itemised. I gather one or two pieces are worth something, but by no means all of it. What is valuable is this little lot." He lifted the top tray of the jewelry case and picked up a stiff envelope. From this he shook on to the table about thirty or forty gold sovereigns. "Did you know she had these?"

"No. Nor apparently did her murderer."

"I agree. Which makes it almost certain that he was not a professional burglar. If he took anything at all, it was only cash. I gather your aunt used to keep a fair amount around the house?"

Gil nodded. "She was eccentric in several ways. Money was one of them. She would cash enormous cheques and hide the money around the house."

"Perhaps forgetting where she'd put it?"

"I don't think ever."

"We've found about fifty pounds in various places with indications that other amounts may have been taken from their hiding-place."

"It sounds as if the murderer may have been disturbed," Gill remarked, shooting Pitcher a quick glance.

"Possibly he was. By Mrs. Isaacs."

Pitcher let his gaze go round the room. Once it had been richly furnished, but now it was shabby. The gold patterned wallpaper was faded where the sun had played on it, the saxe blue carpet showed signs of wear, as did the arms of the sofa on which he was sitting. A glass-fronted cabinet was stuffed with nick-nacks, some of which might be valuable. There was a small bookcase containing a leather-bound set of Tennyson and, incongruously on the shelf below, a row of paperback thrillers.

His gaze came back to the man sitting opposite him, about whom he knew little but was intent on learning more. He knew that he was 34 years old and lived alone in a one-room flat in Swiss Cottage—and that was about all.

"How often used you to see your aunt?" he asked, leaning forward again with the same watchful expression.

"About once a month."

"Was that always here?"

"Yes. I'd call her and suggest a visit." He paused and with a small sour smile added, "And she'd agree, though without much enthusiasm."

"You weren't particularly close to each other?"

"No. But I was her only surviving relative and I felt I had an obligation to keep in touch and make sure she was all right."

"When was the last time you saw her?"

"About a week before her death."

"Here?"

"Yes, always here."

"How long would you stay on these visits?"

"Seldom more than an hour. I usually arrived around four o'clock and we'd have a cup of tea and talk a bit. Sometimes she'd be particularly grumpy and I'd leave sooner."

"Your own parents are dead, I gather?"

"Yes. They were killed by a flying bomb when I was only four years old. I was brought up in the country by the family to whom I'd been evacuated. My aunt made all the arrangements." He gave Pitcher another of his small sour smiles. "She was never fond of children and that's why she kept me at arms' length even after my parents' death."

"Was it your mother or father who was related to Mrs. Isaacs?"

"My mother. She and Aunt Florence were sisters."

"And one more question about your family, when did Mr. Isaacs die?"

"Oh, a long time ago. I'd say about fourteen or fifteen years. He was a nice old boy. I got on with him much better than with my aunt."

"I'd like to ask you now a few questions about the running of this place. What staff did she have?"

"A cleaning woman who came in two mornings a week. I'm afraid I don't recall her name."

Pitcher examined his notebook. "Mrs. Rawlings?"

"Yes. And apart from her, there were the odd job people she employed in the garden. Latterly it was this youth Frensham."

"Yes, we know about him," Pitcher said quickly. He got on well with Nick Attwell and felt affronted by what had happened. Apart from other considerations, it had left him with two sergeants in his team who were older than himself and one of them rather less zealous than he would have wished. From the outset he'd had Paul Frensham very much in his sights, even though it was now going to be much more difficult to interrogate him satisfactorily. He would need to liaise with the A.10 officer investigating Frensham's complaint against Nick before taking any positive step. "So it was just Mrs. Rawlings and Frensham?" he added.

"Yes. As you've seen the house is a bit of a pig-sty. It was far too large for one person, but you probably know how obstinate old people can be about moving. She'd lived here for thirty years and nothing was going to shift her."

"It must be a very valuable property."

"It was valued at eighty thousand pounds a couple of years ago, not that it would fetch that to-day."

"Tell me about this tenant Mrs. Isaacs had in the flat at the top of the house?"

"Derek Unsworth you mean?" Gill's expression reflected distaste. "He was only here three months and then my aunt threw him out."

"There was a row, I believe?"

"I assumed there was though my aunt was strangely tight-lipped about it. Just said she'd had occasion to terminate his tenancy."

"But didn't he depart overnight so to speak?"

"I assume she forewent her rent and he agreed to leave immediately."

Pitcher frowned for a moment or two and then gave a shrug. "It all sounds a bit odd and now we can't find Unsworth. I don't suppose you know where he went?"

Gill shook his head. "No, as I say, my aunt just told me he'd gone and refused to discuss the matter. Mind you, she could be like that. If she decided to make a subject taboo, that was it. And she'd shut you up very smartly if you broached it again."

"Was Unsworth the first and only occupant of the flat?"

"Yes. The conversion was one of her madder ideas. I think she thought it'd bring her in a bit of money, which she didn't need anyway, and also that if she found the right sort of tenant, he or she would be able to do odd jobs for her. I believe that was at the back of her mind. Certainly Unsworth was a blue-eyed boy at the beginning. Then he blotted his copy-book in some way and the next thing he was out on his ear."

"I gather you used to see him when you visited?"

"Not every time, but quite often."

"What was your impression of him?"

Gill's mouth tightened. "I think he was somebody on the make. To be truthful, I wasn't at all happy about his presence here."

"You thought he might try and exert some sort of influence over your aunt?"

"Something like that, yes."

"But you've no evidence that he ever did?"

"None. Though the mystery of his sudden departure remains."

"We must re-double our efforts to find him," Pitcher said in a decisive tone.

"You think he might have killed my aunt?"

"It's much too soon to say. He's in the frame and therefore I'm interested in him. We have no evidence that he ever came back here after leaving and that was two weeks before Mrs. Isaacs' death."

Pitcher's normal expression was one of quiet watchfulness. Though his mind reacted swiftly, his face seldom reflected emotion. Occasionally there would be a quick shy smile, but most times his only response would be a slight closing or wider opening of his very clear grey eyes.

He now gave Gill a rare smile.

"Let me prepare my next question by saying that the police always like to have witnesses confirm what may already be obvious. The question is this: was there ever any suggestion that you might move into the flat upstairs?"

"Not from my aunt."

"And on your part."

"No."

"How did Unsworth come to take it?"

"She advertised it in the local paper."

Pitcher was thoughtful for a moment. "You've been very patient, Mr. Gill, and I think I have only one more question to ask you at the moment. Did your aunt's will come as a surprise to you?"

The corners of Gill's mouth went abruptly down; then meeting Pitcher's gaze, he said, "I obviously hoped I'd be left more than a hundred pounds, which I can only regard as conscience money on her part." His tone was bleak and his expression reflected sudden anger. "After all, I was her only surviving relative and I tried to fulfill a nephew's duty toward a widowed aunt." He stuck his chin out in a gesture of defiance. "I think I'm entitled to feel bitter. After all, I regard myself as a more meritorious object than the half dozen charities which are going to benefit."

"She had never given you any inkling?"

"She never mentioned her will to me. I assumed she had made one as once or twice she referred to all her affairs being looked after by her bank manager. He gets five hundred pounds, I gather." He suddenly slumped back in his chair. "Quite frankly I had no idea how I stood. In my most optimistic moods, I used to kid myself that I'd probably inherit everything or, at least, be the major beneficiary. In what I thought of as my more realistic moments, I used to reckon on a substantial legacy. A few thousand pounds say." He shook his head wearily. "But I obviously wasn't realistic enough."

Pitcher rose and straightened the front of his jacket. "I just want to go up to your aunt's bedroom for another quick look around. If you care to wait a few minutes, I can give you a lift." As he made his way upstairs, Detective Chief Inspector Pitcher reflected on the man he had been interviewing. By all accounts, Mrs. Isaacs had been a difficult old lady. On the other hand, Pitcher found he had formed a few reservations about her nephew. The thinning sandy hair and the weak jaw line, in conjunction with the silver-buttoned blue blazer and club tie, produced the identikit of a minor con-man. He might be misjudging the man and certainly if he were in any way a con-man, he had singularly failed to con his aunt. Pitcher was too intelligent to reach snap judgments of people, as he knew how often they could be wrong. An open mind was all important at this stage of an investigation.

He reached the top of the stairs and crossed the broad landing to the door of Mrs. Isaacs' bedroom which looked out over the garden at the back.

It was a large room, full of heavy furniture, including an old-fashioned washstand with a marble top and on it a jug and bowl decorated with pink roses.

A mahogany double bed with a heavy grey silk cover reaching all round to the floor dominated the room.

It had been at the foot of this bed that Mrs. Isaacs had been found dead from multiple fractures of her skull. She had lain there until discovered by Mrs. Rawlings the next morning.

The pathologist reckoned that she had been dead for between twelve and eighteen hours which put her time of death at between 3 and 9 p.m. the previous day.

Such a wide margin added greatly to the difficulties facing the police in seeking to eliminate any suspect.

The reddish brown stain on the mushroom pink carpet showed where her head had lain. The under-felt and the floor boards which were also stained indicated just how long she had lain there bleeding.

Over against the fireplace stood a cast-iron King Charles spaniel, intended as a rest for poker and fire tongs. It had a forlorn, lonely look, as well it might. Its companion had been carefully wrapped in polythene and labelled and taken to the laboratory for examination, for it had been used as the weapon of murder. Unfortunately, its surface had revealed only smudged and unidentifiable finger-prints, so that was yet another frustrated trail.

For a while, Pitcher gazed about him to make sure that nothing had been overlooked. The doctors, the scientists, the photographers and the finger-print people had long since come and gone. His own officers had been through every drawer and looked under and behind every piece of furniture. The net result had been depressingly negative.

His gaze returned to the heavily stained carpet and to the chalk outline showing how the body had lain. With only a minimum effort of recollection, he could envisage the scene as he had originally viewed it. It had been a clumsy but vicious attack. Whoever it was had over-reacted. Any one of the blows would have sufficed to kill her, the pathologist said.

The room had been in disarray as if someone had searched for something. But what? Money perhaps, but certainly not jewelry. Two diamond rings had been left on her fingers, a cameo brooch was still pinned to her blouse. Her earrings had fallen off during the attack. One had been found on the floor not far from where she lay. It was a green one. Now he came to think of it he hadn't seen the other. It may have got lost among her clothing.

He crossed to the window and looked out. Oliver Gill was standing on the uneven patch of lawn staring into the middle distance. He looked slight and defenceless and Pitcher wondered if his first judgment had been too harsh.

Overgrown laurels abutted the grass and a cinder path ran round the perimeter. Whatever tidying up Paul Frensham did was not very apparent.

17

So far he was the only person known to have been at the house on the afternoon when Mrs. Isaacs died, assuming her death to have occurred nearer 3 than 9 p.m.

It was significant, too, that Frensham had made this allegation against Detective Sergeant Attwell—as if attack was the best form of defence.

It was with such thoughts in mind that Pitcher returned downstairs. There was nothing further to be done at the house.

The open jewel case still rested on the table in the drawing-room. A quick look satisfied Pitcher that its contents had remained undisturbed.

Chapter 3

Detective Chief Superintendent Upperton was nearing the end of his tour of duty with A.10, the branch at Scotland Yard that was responsible for investigating complaints against police. His stint there had done nothing to reinforce his faith in human nature and he sometimes felt he had reached a point where he didn't believe anyone. Where truth was like a football to be booted in any direction that suited the kicker.

He was a tall, thin, bespectacled man with a slight stoop, who was known as professor to his colleagues.

He had been handed the Frensham complaint and told to get on with it quickly. Within an hour he had phoned the Frensham home in Finchley, where, unfortunately, he had found himself speaking to Sir Guy Frensham.

His suggestion that Paul Frensham should call at the Yard in order that a full statement setting out his complaint could be taken was peremptorily brushed aside.

"My son is still considerably shaken by his experience with Sergeant Attwell and a visit to Scotland Yard will not be conducive to

19

your obtaining a proper statement from him," Sir Guy had said briskly. "If you want to see him free of any psychological pressures, you must come out here. Now, when'll you come?"

Upperton had the tact to remain silent on the possibility of paternal, as opposed to psychological, pressures being present and had said he would come immediately.

At this Sir Guy had given a small condescending laugh and said that his son was out and would not be home till dinner time. He had further given the impression that the Frenshams did not receive police officers in their house at unsocial hours.

Thus it was that Upperton made an appointment to call the following afternoon—the morning also being inconvenient for some unspecified reason—and arrived at the house in Finchley at about the same time as Detective Chief Inspector Pitcher was interviewing Oliver Gill less than a couple of miles away.

The two houses, however, could not have been less alike. The Frenshams' was post-war Georgian with a well-kept garden, a heated swimming-pool and a double garage in which Upperton noted a black Mercedes and a Volvo, each bearing this year's registration letter. In the drive was a small and slightly older Fiat which was presumably Paul's.

The sight of the cars did nothing to raise Upperton's spirits. With Detective Sergeant Young at his side he approached the front door and rang the bell. A melodious chime echoed within.

The door was opened by a tall, blonde girl with a grave expression.

"Please enter," she said, "Sir Guy is expecting you. He is in his study. Come this way, please."

"Our appointment is with Mr. Paul Frensham," Upperton said, though realising that was unlikely to alter the course of events.

"Sir Guy will speak to you first," the girl said, leading the way across the hall to a white-painted door on the right. She opened it without knocking and announced, "Here are the policemen."

Sir Guy Frensham waited until they were inside the room before getting up from behind his desk. He looked just as he did on T.V., the luxuriant growth of carefully tended silvery hair with just a suspicion of a wave in it, the perennial sun tan, the very blue eyes.

"Come in, gentlemen," he said expansively, taking off the pair of heavy-rimmed spectacles which were also well known to his T.V. audience. "I'll turn my son over to you in a few minutes, but I thought I'd like to have a few words with you first." He paused and assumed the portentous expression which always prefaced one of his man-to-man utterances. "I'm glad to hear that Sergeant Attwell has been suspended from duty. His sort bring no credit on the force. As the Commissioner is well aware, the police have no stauncher friend than myself. On the other hand, both when I was in parliament and now as a so-called television personality, there has never, as I'm sure you know, been a stronger opponent of corruption in public life or a more energetic fighter for the rights of those less able than some to look after themselves."

He looked from Upperton to Young as if to obtain confirmation of this unexceptionable statement. But Upperton merely blinked and Sergeant Young gazed back with impassivity.

"Of course I'm not asking for my son to be treated differently from anyone else, just that you investigate his allegation thoroughly and assure me at the end that justice has been done, however disagreeable the consequences to Scotland Yard's reputation. I may say that it was shock enough to my son to be told that he had been working in this old woman's garden on the day she met her death without subsequently being threatened with arrest unless he met your Sergeant Attwell's demand for a bribe." He walked across to the door. "I have to go out for half an hour, so you can talk to Paul in here. My wife's resting upstairs and the two younger children are at a party."

"Was the girl who opened the door your daughter?" Upperton enquired.

"No such luck," Sir Guy said with a resonant laugh. "She's our Swedish au pair, Kerstin Borg, pronounced Sherstin, but known to us all as Kersty. Sweet girl, isn't she? We'd be lost without her. She looks after my two youngest, Jane who is four and Jason who is six. There are also Robert, ten, and Sally who is fourteen. They're at boarding-school. Paul's the eldest. He's just left school." He gave them one of his embracing smiles. "I've quite a spread-out family as you've gathered."

No wonder his wife's resting, Young thought to himself.

He opened the door. "Kersty," he called out. "Go and ask Paul to come down, will you?"

While they waited, Upperton glanced around the study. A long settee in white buckskin ran the whole length of one wall. On the opposite side of the room the wall had book shelves from floor to ceiling. There seemed to be a great number of reference books and also a lot of novels. To Upperton who, despite his scholarly appearance, scarcely ever read a book, they were just novels. He suspected, and in fact correctly, that they were fashionable books which the man about town would be expected to have read. Apart from the desk, whose top resembled one of those shiny black floors on which Fred Astaire and Ginger Rogers used to dance, and was, moreover, large enough for the purpose, the only one item of furniture was a huge television set.

The door opened and a young man came in. He was wearing sandals, blue jeans and a yellow T-shirt with "Chicago Ramblers" inscribed across the front and beneath the writing a picture of a figure on a motorcycle.

He had dark curly hair, full lips and a sullen expression.

Sir Guy Frensham put an arm round his son's shoulders.

"Paul, these are the two gentlemen from Scotland Yard who've come to take a statement from you. I want you to tell them everything that happened when Sergeant Attwell called here. Don't keep anything back. There's nothing to be afraid of. Attwell can't harm you and it's your duty to put everything on record." He gave his son's back an encouraging pat. "I'll leave you with them, but I'll be back in about half an hour." He turned to Upperton. "I'll see you on my return, Chief Superintendent."

"Sit where you want," Paul Frensham said in an off-hand tone as he moved across and seated himself in the desk chair, swivelling it round and putting his feet up on the edge of the desk.

After a second's hesitation, Upperton and Young sat down on the long settee. They had the impression of being voluptuously enveloped in a sea of white blancmange. After a small unsuccessful attempt to sit upright, Upperton struggled to his feet, while Paul Frensham watched him with an expression of mild disdain.

"The best thing will be for you to tell us the whole story, Paul, starting at the beginning and going right through to the end and then we'll turn it into a written statement which you can sign. That way we can record the essentials on paper and not waste time writing down a lot of irrelevances."

"O.K.," Paul Frensham said, as though the whole thing was a matter of indifference to him. "It happened on Wednesday. Everyone was out except for me when this fellow of yours, Attwell, comes knocking at the door."

"What time was this?"

"I'd say about three-thirty. I know my father was at the studio all that day and my mother hadn't got back from a lunch date and Kersty had gone to collect Jason from school and taken Jane with her. So as I say, I was alone. When I opened the front door, this fellow Attwell more or less pushed himself inside. He asked me if I was Paul Frensham and when I said I was, he asked me if I'd been working at Mrs. Isaacs' place the previous afternoon? I told him I had and asked him what his questions were in aid of."

"Had he told you that he was a police officer?" Upperton broke in.

"I think he had. I'm not too sure. It was about then that he told me, anyway." He paused with a thoughtful expression. "Yes, he must have told me, because I was beginning to wonder if he mightn't be an imposter. He was so aggressive and intimidating, I didn't think he could be a genuine policeman. He'd pushed me up against the wall and was more or less pinning me there. But he produced some sort of identity card which showed he was a detective sergeant. He asked me what I knew about Mrs. Isaacs' death. I *ask* you, what a question! I didn't even know the old girl was dead. But that really scared me, particularly when he went on to say that I was wanted at the station for questioning. I tried to tell him that I must ring my father, but he just wouldn't listen." He shook his head as though in painful recollection, while Upperton leaned against the bookshelves watching him. "All I can say is that he behaved very differently from the sort of policeman I've been brought up to respect." He glanced quickly from one officer to the other with an almost bored expression. His voice too had been colourless without any hint of emotion. It was difficult to believe that he ever got any fun out of living. "When I said I must go upstairs first, he insisted on coming too. I told him he had no right but he just came. And once inside my bedroom, he began searching the place. He opened drawers and looked everywhere. Then he went into my bathroom and he found a sweater hanging up to dry and he wanted to know why it had been washed. Said he wanted to take it away for examination."

"Did you agree?"

"Are you joking? I didn't agree to anything. He just did as he wanted. It would have needed a regiment of Guards to have stopped him."

"What happened after that?"

"Questions, that's what happened. He threw questions at me until I didn't know my head from my arse. Questions all about what I did at Mrs. Isaacs the previous afternoon. Where I went, who I saw. All the time trying to trick me and finally dragging me off to the police station."

"Was he alone?"

"Yes."

"He drove you to the station?"

"Yes."

"Where did you sit in the car?"

"In the front passenger seat."

"I see." Upperton's tone was strictly neutral, but his meaning was not lost on Paul Frensham.

"By that time I was so scared, I was like a jelly," he remarked in a truculent tone. "You don't know what it's like to be at the receiving end of one of your bully boys' attentions."

"What happened in the car?" Upperton asked dispassionately.

Letting out a slight belch, Frensham frowned for a second or two.

"It was in the car that his attitude suddenly changed. He said I was a strong suspect for the murder and that it didn't need much more to clinch the case against me."

"Yes?" Upperton urged in the sudden silence that followed. Both officers were observing him intently and this seemed to be making him uneasy.

Still frowning he went on, "He then suddenly said that he'd discovered a vital piece of evidence which told against me. He said nobody else knew of it and that he would withhold it if I made it worth his while." He passed a tongue across his lips. "He said he knew my father was a wealthy man and would be willing to pay to avoid a scandal."

"Go on."

"He said that two thousand pounds wasn't too much in the circumstances. He told me to think about it and let him know quickly."

"And what did you say to all this?"

"I told him he must be talking nonsense as there couldn't be any evidence against me and that I'd report him. He just laughed and said it would be word against word and no one was likely to accept mine. And he told me to think again and to think hard as there wasn't much time. And then I suddenly realised that he meant to plant evidence on me and I became even more scared. I told him he must give me a bit of time. Just after that we arrived at the station and I didn't see him again until just before I left. He came into the room where I was waiting and said, 'I'll give you till to-morrow, sonny.' And that was the last I saw of him."

"I gather from what you have told us that Sergeant Attwell wasn't present when you were interviewed at the police station?"

"No, it was two other officers."

"How long were you at the station?"

24

"About an hour to an hour and a half."

"Did you tell anyone about Sergeant Attwell's conduct?"

"My mind was in a turmoil. I didn't know what to do."

"So you didn't tell anyone?"

"I've explained why I didn't," he said with a renewed note of truculence.

"Who brought you home?"

"A police car with a couple of uniformed officers in it."

"And then at some point, you told your father what had happened?"

"Yes, when he got back that night. He phoned Scotland Yard immediately."

"Did you tell anyone else before your father returned? Your mother?"

Frensham hesitated. "I told Kersty. There was no point in telling my mother. She wouldn't have known what to do."

Upperton nodded slowly. "In a moment, we'll start getting that down on paper in statement form. But before we do so, I want to be absolutely clear that you realise the gravity of your allegation. . . ."

"Of course I do."

"If you'll let me finish. You are alleging that Sergeant Attwell solicited a bribe of two thousand pounds from you. Not only that, but he threatened to fabricate evidence against you if you didn't comply."

"That's right," Frensham said with a bored shrug.

"You realise that to make false accusations against the police is itself a criminal offence if they result in a waste of police time?"

"Whose side are you meant to be on? I thought you were here to investigate my complaint." Frensham's tone was hostile.

"That's precisely what I'm here to do. But it's also my job to satisfy myself that you're aware of all the implications of what you're alleging."

"Well, you can be satisfied," Frensham said rudely.

"Right. While Sergeant Young is taking down your statement, I should like to have a word with Miss Borg. Where can I find her?"

Paul Frensham stared at Upperton with suspicion.

"I don't know if she's in."

"She was a short time ago. Just go to the door and call her, would you?"

Scowling, Frensham removed his feet from his father's desk and went over to the door. As he opened it, Upperton caught sight of Kerstin hurrying down the short passage which, he presumed, led to the kitchen.

"Miss Borg," he called out, darting through the door. She turned her head and he went on, "I wonder if I might have a word with you. Where would be a convenient place?"

For a few seconds she stared at him impassively. "In this room if you wish," she said, leading the way into a breakfast alcove adjoining the kitchen.

"Paul says that he told you of what took place between himself and Sergeant Attwell," Upperton said as he followed her through the door. "What exactly did he tell you?"

"This policeman who asked him for money, you mean?" she enquired. "Poor Paul, he was so frightened when he came home. He just wanted to tell me everything."

"But what did he tell you, Miss Borg?"

"He has not told you?" she asked with a puzzled expression.

"Yes, he has. I just want to know what he told you?"

"Ah-ah! Now I understand. You wish to check. But why? Do you not believe what he has told you?"

Upperton let out a sigh. "Miss Borg, I don't know anything about police investigations in Sweden, but in England we try and corroborate what a witness has said. You understand the word, corroborate?"

"I understand it, but can't say it," she said with a small smile.

"Yes, well, we try and find confirming evidence is what it amounts to."

"I see. Well, this policeman asks Paul for two thousand pounds, otherwise he will make sure that Paul is accused."

"That's what Paul told you?"

"Of course."

"Was anyone else in the house when Paul told you this?"

"Perhaps Lady Frensham, but not Sir Guy."

"And what did you say?"

"I said he must tell his father when he comes home."

"Were you here when he got home the previous afternoon?"

The girl frowned. "I do not understand."

"He had been working at Mrs. Isaacs' the previous afternoon, I was wondering if you saw him when he arrived back?"

"I do not remember," she replied with a distinct note of hostility. "Sometimes I am here, sometimes I am not. I do not keep a record of when I see Paul."

"I wouldn't expect you to," Upperton replied mildly. "But I gather your answer is that, if you did see him, you have no reason now to recall the occasion?"

"You are puzzling me. I am not used to English police inquisitions."

"Not an inquisition, please, Miss Borg. Just a few questions aimed at the truth. Did Paul ever speak to you about Mrs. Isaacs?"

"And what is the relevance of that to your enquiry into my son's complaint?" The tone was icy and Upperton turned to find Sir Guy Frensham standing in the doorway wearing an expression of Olympian displeasure.

"Anything that helps to support your son's allegation is material to my enquiry," Upperton replied, uncowed.

"I wouldn't dispute that, but it hardly answers my question." His voice hardened. "I trust you are not going to give me cause to express dissatisfaction with the manner in which you are conducting your investigation. I will not tolerate your taking advantage of a young foreign girl who is a guest in my house by asking her questions which by no stretch of imagination can be relevant and which indicate that you suspect my son of being implicated in some way in the death of this old lady. Do I make myself clear?"

"I am sorry that such an innocent question should have so annoyed you," Upperton said calmly.

"You are being tendentious and not a little impertinent," Sir Guy retorted. "But let me make something else clear before you leave. If the officers investigating the murder wish to interview my son further, they will do so only by appointment and in the presence of my solicitor. You may like to convey that to those concerned. I do not propose to have my son treated like some seventeen-year-old scally-wag they've picked up in the street for loitering with intent."

Upperton said nothing. There was much he would like to have said, but nothing which might not land him in trouble. If he had been closer to retirement, he might have risked it. As it was, silence was the only safe course. It was, at least, he reflected, instructive to have seen the urbane T.V. personality with his populist appeal in a different role.

A few minutes later, Sergeant Young had finished taking down Paul Frensham's statement. Sir Guy read it with an imperious frown on his face before allowing his son to sign it.

As soon as the officers had been ushered off the premises and his father in a display of considerable ill humor had shut himself away in his study, Paul Frensham ran quickly upstairs to the room at the top of the house occupied by Kerstin Borg.

Without knocking he opened the door and went in. Kersty, who was standing in the middle of the floor, glanced up without any sign of pleasure at his arrival. He went over and, with a faint smirk, kissed her on the lips. She remained motionless and stared at him dispassionately as he stepped back from her.

"That's got rid of them," he said with a further smirk. "Everything's going to be all right. What's wrong, Kersty, why are you looking at me as if I'd just made a puddle on the floor?"

"You are so young, Paul," she said in a tone of faint irritation. "Just because I have taught you how to make love properly does not mean you know everything. I am worried for you."

He looked at her, his head on one side, a what-have-I-done-now expression on his face.

"You see, you are just a little boy when you look like that. You must grow up, Paul. Grow up quickly. Do not be deceived by your own cleverness."

"What about *your* own cleverness?"

She studied him gravely for a full half minute. Paul wished he could read her thoughts, but she was particularly adept at concealing them when she wanted. He had never really discovered what she was thinking when they were in bed together. Her body could perform with passion, but somehow her mind never seemed to become wholly involved in their love-making. Come to think of it, neither did his, but he didn't regard that as out of the ordinary.

She made a move toward the door.

"Where are you going?" he asked with a note of faint anxiety.

"I have to fetch Jason from a party."

He put out a hand and held her by the wrist.

"May I come to you to-night?"

"Perhaps. Now I must go." She shook her hand free and gave his cheek a light pat. "I must think—for both of us."

Chapter 4

Clare was able to manage with considerably less sleep than her husband. This had certainly been an advantage when she'd been in the force and it was still one with a baby in the house.

She was already up and dressed by the time Nick woke the next morning. For a split second, he couldn't think why this day was different from others, just that it was. Then recollection flooded in and with it a renewed sense of despair.

A few moments later, Clare came in with a mug of tea.

"I've been thinking," she said—in fact she had lain awake thinking for a large part of the night—"and wondering how you propose to pass the time while you're suspended." She noticed him wince at the word. "Look, darling, we've got to be able to talk about it without your reacting as though I've said something in bad taste."

"I know," he said with a nod. "So what have you been wondering?"

"What I said: how are you proposing to pass the time?"

"I expect there are various odd jobs to be done about the house," he said, gloomily.

"There are, but not enough to keep you busy for long. Anyway, I've got a better idea."

"What's that?"

"Take on Simon full time."

"How do you mean, full time?"

"Get him up in the morning and attend to his needs until it's time to put him to bed in the evening." She observed his dubious expression and added, "After all, how often have you said that you don't see enough of him, that he'll grow up regarding his father as a stranger? Here's your chance to remedy that."

"But what are you going to do?"

"Oh, I shall probably be around most of the time, but I shan't be tied. I'll be able to come and go with a freedom I've not known for ten months." She gave him an affectionate smile. "Don't look so un-enthusiastic. After all, you're very good with him and I'm sure you'll both benefit from the change of routine."

"When do I start?"

"Now. I told him you'd be with him in a couple of minutes."

As if to underline the message, Simon let out a sudden howl for attention.

Though Clare's plan seemed fairly obvious, it was the result of considerable thought. The object at all costs was to keep him busy and Simon would certainly see to this. If Nick didn't have enough to do, he would inevitably brood more deeply over his plight. It would be difficult to avoid self-pity and Clare could foresee the strains which would be placed on their day-to-day life. It wasn't that she feared for their marriage. She was blithely confident that it would survive what-ever the outcome. It was the short-term prospects which worried her much more.

What she proposed to get up to during her new-found freedom was her concern.

She had just finished making the bed when Nick appeared in the doorway carrying a contented-looking Simon.

"I'll just go out and do some shopping," she said. "For once, I'll be ahead of the crowds."

She gave her husband and son a kiss each and departed from the room.

By the time she had finished her shopping it was nine o'clock and she decided it was not too early to make the telephone call which was the main object of her outing.

There was a public kiosk about fifty yards from the supermarket which had somehow managed to survive the attention of vandals. Clare shut herself in and dialled the number she had written down on a scrap of paper the previous evening.

"May I speak to Miss Macpherson please?" she said when a voice answered at the other end.

"This is Miss Macpherson," the voice replied warily. "Who are you?"

"My name's Clare Attwell, I believe you met my husband in Westminster Abbey yesterday afternoon in somewhat unusual circumstances. He told me all about it and I'd be very grateful if you and I could meet."

"Well, I'm not really sure. . . ." Alice Macpherson said in a still wary tone.

"Oh I'm not on the warpath or anything," Clare said quickly with a small nervous laugh. "I gather you know this youth who's made a complaint against my husband and I'd like to ask you a bit more about him. I don't know whether Nick mentioned it but I was in the police myself before I became married."

"Yes, he told me. The thing is, Mrs. Attwell, I really don't think I can be of any help. I met Paul Frensham only once and I've already told your husband what little I know about him."

"Nevertheless, I should be so grateful if we could meet for a talk. Any time, any place, convenient to you. But as soon as possible."

"I could get away for a couple of hours this afternoon if that's any help."

"Splendid. Where would suit you?"

"It'd better be near here."

"You name somewhere."

"There's a teashop run by two middle-aged ladies in smocks. It's called Paradise Regained. I can't remember the name of the street but it's about a hundred and fifty yards from Hampstead tube station. I could be there about half-past three."

"That'll be wonderful. I'll see you then and I am most grateful."

It was with a feeling of elation that Clare left the kiosk and returned home. She found Nick lying on his back on the sitting-room floor while Simon delightedly pounded at his father's tautened stomach with his tiny fists.

"He's really getting quite strong," Nick said admiringly.

"As long as you don't encourage him to do that to me," Clare remarked.

"What are you going to do now?" he asked, propping himself up on his elbows.

"Clean up the kitchen and do a bit of washing. Incidentally, Simon's well on the way to disproving every T.V. advert within his experience. It would seem that he is the only child in Britain not prepared to burgle the Bank of England's vaults looking for Crane's blackcurrant Supermousse. Instead he empties the lot down his front which in turn completely defeats the magical properties of New Everest Super-White washing powder."

Nick laughed. "You'd better put Messrs. Crane in touch with the makers of New Everest and leave them to fight it out."

"And meanwhile feed Simon by means of intravenous drip," Clare said cheerfully. "Why don't you take him out for a walk? There are some squirrels on the common whose antics he's become interested in."

Not long after Nick and Simon had left the house, the phone rang.

"Clare? This is Bob Lucas. I was ringing to see how Nick was."

Detective Sergeant Lucas was a friend and colleague of Nick's in C.1 at the Yard.

"He's out at the moment, Bob. I've sent him and Simon off for a walk."

"It's a diabolical thing to have happened, Clare. How's he taken it?"

"More or less as you'd expect. It's obviously shaken him to the core and the problem is going to be keeping up his morale. How long do you think it'll be, Bob, before he knows the result of the investigation?"

Sergeant Lucas sighed. "I wish I could give you cheerful news on that Clare, but you know how these enquiries drag, even though this one is obviously due for some prompt treatment. Incidentally, you can tell Nick that the professor has been put in charge of the investigation."

"Who's he?"

"Detective Chief Superintendent Upperton and he has Phil Young as his skipper. They'll make a good team. Obviously hand-picked to deal with that odious man, Frensham. Have you ever seen him on the box, Clare? One of those friends of the people you wouldn't trust to pass you the sugar."

"Can you ring again later, Bob? I know Nick would like to have a talk with you. It's one's friends who count most at times like this."

"I wish I'd seen him yesterday. But I gather he walked straight out of the building as soon as he left the Commander's room. By the time I heard the news, he'd gone."

"He told me he hadn't wanted to face any of his friends."

"Poor Nick. It's bloody diabolical. Anyway, when do you suggest I call, Clare?"

"Try between two and three. I have to go out soon after two and, with luck, Simon'll be asleep so you shouldn't be interrupted."

By the time Nick and Simon returned, Clare had prepared lunch.

"We'll have it a bit early, darling, as I want to go out this afternoon."

"Where are you going?"

"I thought it'd be an opportunity to go and see Helen, and it takes ages to get to her."

Helen was a cousin of Clare's who had recently had a baby herself and who lived on the other side of London. Clare had selected her for this particular white lie as Helen had not yet got a telephone in her new flat and there could therefore be no question of Nick trying to phone her there.

"By the way, Bob Lucas rang, but he's going to call again after lunch. He just wanted to have a chat. He says that Detective Chief Superintendent Upperton and Detective Sergeant Phil Young are investigating the complaint."

"Oh!" Nick's expression became suddenly closed in. But at that moment, Simon whom he was holding under one arm gave a protesting wriggle and almost slipped from his grasp. Turning away, Clare reflected that Simon was probably the only person who could successfully distract his father's mind from his problems. It was a risk she was prepared to run that, at the end of it all, their son would have become used to a great deal more attention than he normally received when he was alone with his mother. After all, as Sir Guy Frensham had himself said in a recent cloying programme, "Whatever the benefit accruing to one person, somewhere there has to be a corresponding loss." At the time, Clare had regarded it a typical piece of sententious philosophising of a sort that television specialises in. She still thought it spurious, even though it had its application to present circumstances.

It was five minutes before half-past three when she walked into Paradise Regained and selected a corner table at the back of the shop. The place was empty and there was a strong smell of recently served lunch. A large poster on one of the walls announced poetry readings every Monday evening.

One of the besmocked ladies emerged from the rear of the shop. She had iron grey hair cut short and with a fringe in front. She didn't look like someone with an interest in poetry, but you could never tell, least of all in Hampstead.

"I'm afraid we're finished serving lunch," she said in a brisk tone.

"Actually, I've arranged to meet a friend for tea. But perhaps I can wait till she comes before ordering."

"Certainly. We serve a nice old-fashioned tea if you like that sort of thing. Buttered scones and jam and cream and assorted cakes. Everything home-made, of course."

"Do many people go in for all that nowadays?" Clare asked in surprise.

"We do an excellent trade, especially on Saturday afternoons."

"What about your poetry readings, are they well attended?"

"There are always about half a dozen regulars. My friend is the poet. I don't often attend myself. Miss Paisley, that's my friend, has had some of her poems published in one of our little local journals."

The door was pushed open and Alice Macpherson came in. She had been outside a few seconds trying to decide whether the rather pretty girl talking to the proprietor could be Clare Attwell. She hadn't known quite what to expect, though her imagination had tended to prepare her for someone looking more school-mistressy. If not actually hair pulled tight back into a bun, at any rate not attractive fair hair falling loosely to the shoulders.

Eventually she had decided that it must be Clare and she entered.

Clare looked up with a hopeful smile. "Miss Macpherson?" The two women shook hands. "It really is good of you to meet me," Clare went on. "And what a perfect choice, it's so quiet. What would you like? I understand they serve an old-fashioned tea. I'm sure you ought to try it if you've never done so."

"Just black coffee for me, Mrs. Attwell."

A few minutes later, they had been served, Alice with coffee and Clare with a pot of tea, and had decided that it would be much more sensible to call each other by their first names.

"I'm sure it goes without saying," Clare began, "but the starting point for me is my complete belief in my husband's innocence." She gave Alice Macpherson a shy glance. "Obviously I'm not asking you to share that belief on such a short acquaintance. On the other hand,

I like to think you wouldn't have agreed to meet me if you'd decided he was guilty."

"I could hardly have decided that anyway," Alice protested. "Let's just say that I'm prepared to go along with what your husband told me."

"Thank you. Knowing that makes it much easier for me." Clare shook her head in a small gesture of disbelief. "You see, it is quite the craziest allegation that anyone's ever made against a police officer, and that's saying something. I'm not saying that policemen haven't solicited and accepted bribes because everyone knows of instances where they have. But it's the first time it's been suggested in a murder case. These things happen, when they happen at all, when you're dealing with the real criminal fraternity who live by their own code of villainy. But that any officer, let alone my own husband, should solicit a huge bribe from a seventeen-year-old youth who is the son of a well-known public figure is the maddest of all mad ideas. Not even the stupidest of bent officers would have tried that one! And my husband is certainly not bent, nor is he that stupid." She paused slightly out of breath. "I mean, he's not stupid at all."

"He certainly didn't strike me as stupid," Alice said, "and I accept that he's not bent, as you put it. All of which means that Paul Frensham must have lied about your husband."

"Exactly," Clare said, her eyes sparkling with excitement in the belief she had found an ally. "The question is why did he lie and the answer must be to throw the police off the scent. He reacted like the squid that sends out a cloud of ink to confuse its enemy."

"But what was the scent he wanted to obscure?"

"That's what we've got to find out, Alice," Clara said eagerly. Then observing Alice's rather dubious expression, she added, "I'm sorry, I didn't mean to sound so patronising. You've been wonderful already and I certainly don't want to drag you further into our troubles. But that brings me to the point of our meeting, can you tell me anything about Paul Frensham which may help to throw light on his behaviour?"

"No, except from all accounts he's capable of behaving like that. He sounds a nasty, spoilt brat." Alice put down her cup and looked Clare in the eyes. "After you phoned this morning, I spoke to my girl-friend who knows Kersty Borg, the Frenshams' Swedish au pair. She met Kersty the other day—since the murder, that is—and she says that she was talking of going home. She asked my friend not to put it around as she hadn't mentioned it to the Frenshams and didn't want them to find out what she had in mind. My friend described her as being in a strange sort of mood, seeming to want to talk but not doing so and reacting tetchily when my friend asked her any questions. My friend . . . why do I keep on calling her my friend, her name's Betsy . . . Betsy had the impression that something had happened between her and Paul Frensham. She made one or two snide remarks about him. Said how callow he was for his age and that she'd had enough of *all* the Frensham children."

"I wonder where that takes us?" Clare remarked in a reflective tone. "It's certainly interesting. Did Betsy say anything else?"

"She mentioned that Paul Frensham has a friend called Tony Rivings," Alice said, once more meeting Clare's gaze. "He's two or three years older than Paul and comes from a very different sort of background. What Betsy said was that there wasn't a member of the Rivings family who hadn't been to prison or, at any rate, been in trouble with the police, including Tony. It seems he used to visit Paul at the Frenshams until Sir Guy learnt about him and then he was forbidden to enter the house and Paul was told to break with him. But he didn't and they used to meet in cafés and the like. There would seem to have been a certain amount of hero-worship on Paul's part."

"Betsy got this from Kersty, I imagine?"

"Yes. Kersty didn't like the Rivings youth either. He'd once made a crude pass at her and she'd slapped him down, but he'd laughed in her face and said he'd have her asking for it yet. She had got his meaning, even though she'd not understood his words, which was how she came to ask Betsy about the expression."

"It's reasonable to suppose," Clare said, after a thoughtful silence, "that Rivings knew Paul Frensham worked for Mrs. Isaacs. And if he did, he doubtless also knew that she was a wealthy old lady with a reputation for leaving money scattered about her house. In fact, it was just ripe for a burglary." She paused. "I wonder if the police know of Rivings' connection with Frensham?"

Alice gave a shrug. "And that's about all I can tell you, Clare."

"Well, it's certainly been worth the journey to Paradise Regained," Clare said. "And if you do happen to learn anything else from Betsy. . . ."

"I'll let you know at once. Incidentally, does your husband know we're meeting?"

Clare shook her head. "I'll probably tell him quite soon, but not just yet." She gave a little laugh. "He'd have locked me in a cupboard if he'd known what I was proposing to do this afternoon."

As they got up to leave, Clare said, "I'm not trying to be a female Sherlock Holmes, but I am determined to see Nick cleared of this allegation and I'm prepared to do anything I can to achieve that."

Chapter 5

Sitting on the edge of the chair, her cheap tweed coat buttoned up to the neck despite the heat of the room, Mrs. Rawlings contrived to look nervous and forbidding at the same time. She had on a head scarf which was knotted so tightly beneath her chin that her cheeks appeared to balloon out.

Detective Chief Inspector Pitcher, who had sent a car to fetch her, was now wondering how he could put her at her ease.

"Would you like a cup of tea, Mrs. Rawlings?" he asked.

"All right," she said, as though doing him a favour.

"I shan't keep you long, but there are one or two matters arising from Mrs. Isaacs' death that I'd like to clear up. I gather you'd worked for her for nearly five years?"

"Five years next January."

"What sort of person was she, Mrs. Rawlings?"

Mrs. Rawlings gave the handle of her handbag a nervous twist.

"She had her funny ways, but she didn't give me no trouble."

"What sort of funny ways?"

"She had her moods, but I didn't take any notice. I just got on with my work."

"Used she to talk to you much?"

"Sometimes."

"I want to ask you what she ever said about three specific people and let me say that whatever you tell me will be treated in confidence. First of all her nephew, Mr. Gill? Did she ever speak to you about him?"

"No, but anyone could tell what she thought of him. She didn't like him and that's for sure."

"How do you know?"

"It stood out, didn't it? She treated him like dirt. I don't know why he put up with it. Well, I can guess why he did; he was her only relative, wasn't he?"

"Did she ever tell you she didn't like him?"

"She didn't have to, did she?"

"Did you like him?"

Mrs. Rawlings looked up sharply. "I didn't see a lot of him, did I? He never gave me no trouble. Anyway, I've always been one for keeping myself to myself."

"A very sound principle, if I may say so, Mrs. Rawlings," Pitcher said with an encouraging smile. Her only response, however, was to stare sternly ahead of her. "I'd like to ask you next about Derek Unsworth?"

"Oh, him!" Her tone was scornful.

"How did he get on with Mrs. Isaacs?"

"Like a house on fire until their row."

"Yes, I've heard of the row. What was it about?"

"Can't tell you, 'cos I don't know. One day he was still her blue-eyed boy and the next time I came, he was packing to leave."

"Did neither of them give you any idea what they'd quarrelled about?"

"No."

"Did he seem upset? Or was he more angry than upset at going?"

"He just said he was leaving and he referred to Mrs. Isaacs as. . . . Well, he called her names."

"What names?" Pitcher urged.

Mrs. Rawlings' expression became even sterner.

"He called her an old bitch."

"Surely Mrs. Isaacs must have said *something* about his departure?"

"She stayed in her room all day until he'd gone. When she came out, she just said, 'Mr. Unsworth's left, Mrs. Rawlings, and he won't be coming back.' And then I suppose she saw my expression 'cos she went on, 'And I don't want you ever to mention his name in my presence.' And I never did. It was none of my business."

"But before that, they'd always seemed very friendly together?"

"If you ask me she made a fool of herself with him. She was easily old enough to be his mother. She treated him like a lap-dog and he purred all over her."

Despite the somewhat confused imagery, Pitcher thought he had a clear enough picture of the relationship which had existed prior to the row. It was the mystery surrounding the row which remained unsolved.

"And you've no idea where Unsworth went when he left?"

"Could be the north pole for all I know!"

"The last person I want to ask you about, Mrs. Rawlings, is Paul Frensham?"

"Only saw him once or twice when I stayed on afternoons."

"How did he and Mrs. Isaacs get on?"

"He wasn't another of her lap dogs if that's what you mean. He just used to tidy up the garden twice a week. At least, that's what he was supposed to do, but, if you ask me, he was as lazy as most boys his age. Sometimes Mrs. Isaacs would shout at him from a window to get on. Once she found him sitting in the drawing-room when he should have been working and she gave him the sharp edge of her tongue."

"What did *you* feel about him?"

"I didn't take much notice of him," she said in her familiarly scornful tone. "I don't have a lot of use for his sort, anyway."

Pitcher tapped his teeth with the end of the pen with which he had been making notes. "That's all been most helpful, Mrs. Rawlings, and leaves me with just one final question. Somebody brutally murdered Mrs. Isaacs, have you any ideas who that somebody might be?"

"Which of them three you mean?"

"Put it this way, do you think any of them would have been capable of murdering her?"

"Yes."

"Which?"

"All of 'em, of course. I felt like murdering her myself sometimes."

"But you never did!"

"No. It depends, which of 'em had the best reason, don't it?"

Pitcher nodded in a non-committal fashion.

"Is there anyone else you can think of who might have had a motive for killing Mrs. Isaacs?"

She shook her head slowly. "It could have been a burglar, couldn't it?"

"It's a possibility."

It was, indeed, a possibility. Certainly, anyone could have got into the house, for one of Mrs. Isaacs' foibles was to leave both the front-door and back-door unsecured in the daytime when she was at home. But if it was a burglar, something told Pitcher that it hadn't been a casual burglar. The evidence so far seemed to indicate that the murderer was in some way associated with his victim.

Shortly after Mrs. Rawlings had departed, the phone rang.

"Pitcher speaking."

"Good evening, Chief Inspector. This is Detective Chief Superintendent Upperton of A.10. I thought I should let you know that I interviewed young Frensham this afternoon in connection with his complaint against Detective Sergeant Attwell."

"Yes, sir?"

"I don't know if and when you're proposing to see him again, but you'd better be aware that his father'll insist on any interview being conducted in the presence of his solicitor."

"Oh! Though I can't say that I'm particularly surprised."

"Obviously our two enquiries must take their separate courses, chief inspector, but I think I can tell you in confidence that I wasn't greatly impressed by young Frensham."

Upperton's tone was as professional as his appearance at that moment. Pitcher had never served under him and knew him only by sight.

"Another thing, chief inspector," Upperton continued, meticulous as always in addressing an officer he didn't know by his rank, "though one I probably have no need to mention to you, is to watch your step when dealing with Sir Guy Frensham. In my estimation he is one of nature's more dangerous animals and you'll be aware of the power he exercises by virtue of his television appearances."

"Yes, sir, I realise the need for care in that direction. Will you be seeing Paul Frensham again?"

"It may become necessary," Upperton said with a faint sigh, "but I devoutly hope not." He paused. "Well, that's all, chief inspector; I have no doubt we shall be in touch again before long."

Pitcher had just put down the receiver when there was a knock on his door and Detective Sergeant Lyle came in. Though two ranks junior to Pitcher, he was six years older than his chief inspector. He had failed his promotion board for inspector and was now unlikely to rise above his present rank. To his credit, he had risen above his disappointment and had not allowed it to affect his work. Pitcher, who had been selected for accelerated promotion, recognised for his part that an officer like Reg Lyle had a fund of practical experience which outmatched his own.

"I've just had Mr. Upperton on the line," Pitcher remarked and went on to tell Lyle what had transpired.

"It's a pity we didn't shake Master Frensham until his teeth rattled when we had the chance," Sergeant Lyle said with feeling. "Instead of releasing him so that he could run home and then snipe at one of us."

Pitcher nodded. "Our difficulty now is getting access to him."

"He's done it on bloody purpose, guvnor."

"He certainly knows a lot more than he's told us. I'm convinced of that."

"Of course he does!" A crafty expression crept across Sergeant Lyle's face. "But we may be able to get at him round a flank. That's what I came to tell you about."

"Go ahead."

"I had an anonymous phone call half an hour ago. It was a woman speaking from a public kiosk. She just said, 'Tony Rivings might be able to help you. He's a friend of Paul Frensham's.' And then she rang off." He shrugged. "She sounded perfectly sane and sensible, even though she refused to give me her name."

"Anyone ever heard of Tony Rivings?" Pitcher asked in a tone of suspended judgment.

"We're trying to find out all we can as quickly as we can. I'm waiting for a call from C.R.O. now. They said they'd ring me back at once if they had anything on him. That could be it now, guvnor," he said as Pitcher's phone rang.

Pitcher lifted the receiver. "Hold on, he's here," he said, passing it to Lyle with a nod.

There followed a series of monosyllabic noises from Sergeant Lyle as he scribbled notes on a sheet of paper, which Pitcher had shoved across the desk at him. Finally he said, "Thanks very much for your help," and dropped the receiver back on its rest.

Pitcher watched him expectantly.

"Anthony Rivings of 26 Filby Street, Muswell Hill," Lyle read out from his notes. "Aged twenty-two with five convictions for dishonesty. There are three other Rivings of the same address, all with previous records."

"One *of those* families," Pitcher observed drily. "I'll have a word with Muswell Hill and find out what they can tell us." He picked up the receiver again and asked for the other station.

This time it was Lyle's turn to listen to a one-sided conversation in which the person at the other end of the line did all the talking.

"The Rivings' are as well known as their records indicate," he said, turning to Lyle when he had finished. "The only member of the family who hasn't been in trouble is a four-year-old daughter, but they expect time to take care of that before long. Tony, it seems, is the only one prone to violence." He glanced at his watch. "I suggest we go calling, Reg."

Twenty minutes later, Lyle was knocking on the door of 26 Filby Street. Pitcher stood at his side.

"Mrs. Rivings?" Pitcher enquired of the woman who opened it.

"Who are you?"

"Police. We'd like a word with your son, Tony."

"Why?" She was a small, wiry woman with platinum blonde hair and a face like a nutcracker. Her voice was as dulcet as a saw thrusting through metal.

"He may be able to help us."

"I've heard that crap before. If you haven't got a warrant for him, he won't come. And I'll get the Council of Civil Liberties on to you if you try anything."

"Look, Mrs. Rivings," Pitcher said in a patient voice, "we haven't come to arrest him, just to talk to him."

"Wait here," she said, after glaring at them in silence for several seconds. She closed the door and they heard her retreating footsteps.

Pitcher was beginning to wonder if she hadn't made fools of them when the door was opened and a young man peered at them with an expression of considerable suspicion. He was powerfully built with a fresh complexion and black curly hair.

A useful man to have on your side in a fight, Pitcher reflected. Rivings' glance went from one officer to the other.

"What is it, gents?" he asked.

"We'd like to have a word with you, Tony," Pitcher said. "Where can we talk?"

"What's it all about?" Rivings repeated, standing his ground in the doorway.

"Paul Frensham. I believe you know him."

"What about Paul?"

"Can we come in or will you come and sit in the car?"

Rivings nodded toward the car. "But no funny business, is it?"

"We're not going to kidnap you if that's what you mean."

He grinned, revealing white, even teeth. "O.K., I trust you. That's my weakness, trusting the law." He turned and shouted into the house, "It's all right, mama, I'm just going to talk to these gents in their car."

Pitcher and Rivings got into the back of the car while Sergeant Lyle took the driver's seat.

"When did you last see Paul Frensham?" Pitcher asked.

"About a week ago maybe," Rivings said in an offhand tone.

"Where?"

"At Jox Disco in Finchley."

"Did Paul say anything about Mrs. Isaacs on that occasion?"

"Not that I recall."

"You obviously know whom I'm speaking about?"

"The old girl Paul worked for?"

"You know she's been murdered?"

"Poor old cow! How'd I know that?"

"You might have read it in the paper or Paul might have told you." A frown formed on Rivings' brow.

"Who told you I was a friend of Paul Frensham's?" he asked, his voice suddenly full of suspicion.

"Who do you think?" Pitcher remarked with a meaning glance.

"If it's that old father of his, he can take a bloody jump at himself. I'm not taking anything from him just because he's out to protect his own precious son's skin."

"You think Sir Guy Frensham may be trying to do that?"

"He thinks he's God Almighty," Rivings said angrily.

Pitcher, for whom the interview had taken an unexpected and seemingly profitable turn, thought hard how he could further exploit the situation.

"If the old guy has told you that I put Paul up to anything, it's a pack of bloody lies," Rivings went on. "I'm not taking any raps for his son."

"It's every man for himself, eh Tony?"

"Too bloody true!"

"I can understand how you feel. It's not nice to be fingered by the father of your friend." Pitcher's tone was quietly insinuating. "But what I'm chiefly interested in is what Paul himself has told you about Mrs. Isaacs' death."

Rivings' expression seemed suddenly to close up. "Look, mister, I don't think I want to talk about this any more."

"I should have thought you'd be keen to let us have your side of the story."

Rivings bit his lip as he looked pensive for a few moments.

"My side of the story is that I don't know anything about what Paul has got up to. And if he's said anything about me, I deny it and you can't prove a bloody thing."

Pitcher gave a small indulgent smile. "Cool it, Tony, I'm not trying to prove anything against you. It's Paul I'm interested in. Paul and old Mrs. Isaacs."

"I can't help you. I don't know nothing."

"You know it's an offence, Tony, to assist anyone to escape prosecution?"

"So what?"

"You could find yourself in that situation over Paul."

"Look, mister, I've said enough for one evening. Give me time to think a bit."

Reluctant as he was to let Rivings go, Pitcher didn't see how he could sustain the interview much longer without disclosing that he knew far less than Rivings clearly supposed.

"Of course being a few years older than Paul, I imagine he always took your lead?"

Rivings immediately bridled. "What are you suggesting? I never put Paul up to nothing."

Pitcher let out a slightly theatrical sigh. "There seem to be two views about your relationship with Paul. The question is, whom does one believe? I'm open to persuasion that you're telling the truth." He paused. "But I can't pretend that I'm persuaded yet. I'm sure Paul has spoken to you since Mrs. Isaacs' death and I'd like to know what he said."

"Come on, Tony," Sergeant Lyle broke in. "The guvnor's treating you right fairly. Do yourself a favour. You don't imagine that Sir Guy Frensham would cover up for you, do you?"

"Sod Sir Guy!"

"Good thinking, so now why don't you answer Mr. Pitcher's question?"

Rivings stared out of the car window with a concentrated frown. When he turned back, Pitcher realised from his expression that they had lost him.

"I've got nothing more to say, mister. I've told you all I know."

He opened the car door and slowly got out as though he half-expected to be restrained.

"Ta-ta!" he called out with an expression of quizzical amusement at finding himself free on the pavement.

"What do you make of him?" Sergeant Lyle asked, as they drove away.

"I'd sooner deal with him than Sir Guy Frensham any day, that's for sure. What he told us was probably true as far as it went, but it didn't add up to much in the end. At one moment I thought we were going to get much more out of him."

Lyle nodded. "I know; when he thought that Paul Frensham had put him in it, he was about to open up, but then he suddenly shut his mouth."

"We must do a bit of delving into their relationship and then we'll have Rivings along for another interview. And next time, we'll put the pressure on."

Soon after they arrived back at the station, Detective Constable Bax entered Pitcher's office. He had been assigned the task of tracing Derek Unsworth, Mrs. Isaacs' one-time lodger.

"I've found out, sir, that he was a clerk in the wages department at the local council offices at the time he was living at 14 Teeling Road. He handed in his notice suddenly about the time he must have departed from Mrs. Isaacs' and left the same week." D.C. Bax studied his notebook. "I've spoken to his various colleagues, but none of them could help apart from a girl called June Dilley. He took her out once or twice and on one occasion, he asked her back to Teeling Road. She didn't meet Mrs. Isaacs, but she said Unsworth in effect told her that he had the old lady eating out of his hand. He showed this girl, June, all over the house as though he owned it."

"Did he tell her what his row with Mrs. Isaacs had been about?" Pitcher asked.

"No. She said that he seemed very put out one day and when she asked him what was wrong, he told her he'd left Mrs. Isaacs' house and had decided to move into another area altogether. He didn't even work out his notice, but went the following day and she hasn't seen him since, though he did phone her about a week later. But it was only to ask her to send on a pair of shoes he kept in the office for when he arrived with wet feet." Pitcher's interest quickened but was dashed as Bax went on, "The address he gave is a dump of a hotel in Holloway Road, run by an old Cypriot woman who scarcely has two words of English to rub together. Unsworth seems to be about the only person who registered under his own name. That is, unless Engelbert Humperdinck, Robin Hood and the Emperor of Japan really have all put up there recently. Anyway, he left the day after Mrs. Isaacs' death and no one knows where he went. I questioned the half dozen other guests staying there. Four spoke no English at all. One was a scatty old girl who insisted I must be bringing her news of her husband who died several years ago and one was a fluffy white-haired old man who told me he was the Archbishop of Canterbury but didn't want people to get to know. And after that, sir, I'm afraid the trail petered out. My enquiry seems to have set up more questions than it's answered," he added gloomily.

"Oh, I don't know! It has confirmed that Unsworth has deliberately gone to ground. Just why, we must find out."

Chapter 6

Derek Unsworth sat on the edge of the bed looking round the cheerless room into which he had just moved. It was his fourth move since he'd left Teeling Road and it certainly wouldn't be his last.

He had fair, wavy hair and a narrow face. Caught at a certain angle, he wasn't bad looking, but his expression all too often was one of glowering petulance.

He had managed to get himself a job as assistant to the stock-room clerk of a local supermarket and was due to start work there the next day. He had said his name was Eric Worth and had taken his room also under this name.

By moving south of the river, he felt he had placed a barrier between himself and events in Teeling Road, N.2.

He had seen his name mentioned in the newspapers as someone whom the police wished to trace and interview and he thanked heaven that there were no photographs of himself in existence. At least he didn't need to disguise his appearance.

His thoughts went to Mrs. Isaacs and he gave the leg of the bed a vicious kick. He felt no pity for what had befallen her. He'd been on to a good thing there until their row. And what a row it had been!

He could see himself now as she had railed at him, using language straight from the gutter, while he had stood facing her with a faintly ironic smile. This had goaded her into actual physical assault and she had pummelled him with her fists which were about as effective as weapons as balls of wool.

But then he, in turn, had become angry when she ordered him to pack his bags and leave immediately, threatening to send for the police if he didn't.

At that point he had tried to quiet her, reason with her, even mollify her, but to no avail. Not that he had immediately given up. For a quarter of an hour after the initial torrent of her fury was spent, he had gone on trying to talk her round. But her attitude had become more and more implacable toward him and finally he had gone upstairs to his room, smarting from the lashing he had received and bitterly resentful of her refusal to reverse her decision.

He had lain awake half the night turning over in his mind the possibility of making it up to her, even though it would involve swallowing his not inconsiderable pride. And when morning had come, he had crept downstairs and stood for a while outside her bedroom door. Then he had knocked gently and tried the handle, only to discover that the door was locked.

"Florence," he had called out in an urgent tone. "Florence, let me speak to you. We were both a bit hasty last night."

He hadn't heard her footsteps, but suddenly the door was flung open and she stood there like some battered but wrathful deity.

"Get out of my house!" she said in a tone full of venom. "And if you ever do anything about what you've found out, I'll make the rest of your life a misery. I'll hound you until you drop. Now get out!" And the door had slammed in his face.

He had returned upstairs burning with indignation at the further vilification.

And, of course, Mrs. Rawlings had to be in the hall when he finally came downstairs to make his departure. He had brushed past her with a single rancorous comment. He had never cared for Mrs. Rawlings and had recently suggested to Mrs. Isaacs that she should employ a more amenable sort of person. The truth was that Mrs. Rawlings had rejected his efforts to be friendly with silent contempt and he had never forgiven her. If there was one thing he could not abide, it was being snubbed by someone to whom he was making a genial approach.

It was like having a bucket of icy water unexpectedly poured right over you.

He got up from the bed and walked over to the window. The street below stretched with dismal sameness in either direction and he quickly turned away.

He shook himself as though to be rid of an old skin which was ready to fall off.

He had already had partial revenge, but it wasn't enough to satisfy him. He felt there must be more he could do to prove that Derek Unsworth was not someone to be trifled with. The question was, what?

He sat down on the edge of the bed again. If there was one person he disliked more than any other in his immediate past, it was Paul Frensham. A nasty, arrogant youth who'd had the effrontery to answer him back when he had once found him in the dining room where he had no right to be. Answer him back by suggesting that he, Unsworth, had as little right as himself and that, with a lodger like him around, Mrs. Isaacs had better count her spoons more regularly.

It would be nice to see *him* put in his place and some of the smooth white icing chipped off that establishment figure father of his.

He passed a hand across his smooth chin. Perhaps he ought to start a beard just to change his appearance slightly. The trouble was, however, if he began to grow one now, it would be noticed much more than if he left his face as it was. And so far the papers had only given his name. There'd been no description of the man whom the police wished to come forward. And even if a description of him were to be published, it would only make him sound like one of those robots created by an identikit.

He decided to go out and have supper. There was a café on the corner of the main road which looked passable.

And while he was eating, he would make up his mind whether or not to make a certain phone call.

Chapter 7

When Clare returned from her meeting with Alice Macpherson, she found Nick staring vacantly at television. Sir Guy Frensham's face filled the screen, but his voice was silent.

"What's happened to the sound?" she asked from the door.

"I turned it down," Nick said dully.

"Why not turn him off altogether?"

He got up and rather like an automaton moved across to the set and switched it off.

"This'll sound silly," he said with a short nervous laugh, "but I turned on especially to hear him and then found I couldn't bring myself to listen. But I still had to watch his face. It was as if I was afraid of hearing what he might say and yet couldn't take my eyes off him." He came over to Clare. "Anyway, I'm glad you're back, darling."

She threw her arms round his neck and kissed him. For a long time they just held each other in a tight hug.

"Simon asleep?" she asked in his ear.

"Yes. I'm afraid I put him to bed a bit early. I wanted to think."

Clare thrust her head back and looked into her husband's face. What she saw made her heart turn over. Anxiety was etched everywhere. Perhaps her therapy had not been the right treatment after all and yet deep down she knew it was. She suddenly realised that the danger lay in the swing of her own words from euphoria to a reflection of his own state of morbid depression. She must be constant and practical; sympathetic without being sentimental. If only it were as easy to follow as to prescribe.

"Let's sit down," she said, disengaging herself from his arms, "and then you tell me what in particular you needed to think about."

"Our future," he said bleakly. "What'll happen if I get thrown out! Whether I'd stay on if I was reduced in rank! How we'll face up to those things if they happen."

Clare took hold of his hand and squeezed it. "Look, Nick, you know you're innocent and I know you are and that's a good starting point for believing that you'll be proved innocent by this enquiry. Sir Guy Frensham may have hypnotised you, but, luckily, he won't have that effect on your superiors. It may take a bit of time to clear your name, but meanwhile you've got to live with your suspension which is a fact of life. Disagreeable, but temporary. If you allow yourself to become overwhelmed by morbid introspection and tidal waves of self-pity, it's going to be hell for both of us."

"I realise that," he said with a deep sigh. "I was all right until this evening and then my thoughts began to take off."

"They'll go on doing so," Clare said. "No use pretending otherwise, but your withdrawal symptoms will become less acute as time goes by." She didn't necessarily believe this but, nevertheless, hoped that it would prove true. "And as we're obviously not going to be able to avoid the subject for most of the time, let's discuss some of the realities, rather than indulge in gloomy speculation about the future. For example," she went on, "Paul Frensham has made a baseless allegation against you. He must have done so for a reason and the reason must be connected with Mrs. Isaacs' death. Agreed so far?"

"But why did he pick on me?"

"Because you were the officer who fetched him to the station."

"I was acting on instructions."

"Oh, I don't mean it was simply because you did that."

"What do you mean?"

"That you must have seen or heard something of great significance when you went to the house. Something that would point to his guilt as the old lady's killer."

Nick shook his head in rejection of the idea. "I know exactly what I saw and heard and there was nothing that pointed to his guilt. Dammit, Clare, it was the very thing I was doing, looking for clues. Apart from the sweater, there was nothing and we shan't know about the sweater until the lab has reported."

"There must have been something else," Clare said patiently. "It's the only logical explanation." Observing Nick's unpersuaded expression, she went on, "Do you agree that the most obvious reason for Frensham's allegation was to get you removed from the investigation?"

"I just wish I knew why!"

"Well, what other explanation is there?"

"I don't know."

"Concentrate, Nick," she said sharply. "If it wasn't to get you taken off the murder enquiry, what was the reason?"

"But it doesn't make sense, Clare," he expostulated. "If you really want to know my view, I think he's a spoilt and thoroughly spiteful youth who decided to get his own back against me for having picked him up and brought him in. He probably didn't realise what the consequences would be. He spun his father a tale simply to show himself as the injured party. Like the girl who's had an enjoyable roll in the hay and then tells her mother she's been raped."

"Possible but unlikely," Clare remarked after a thoughtful pause. "Anyway, accept for the moment that he did make his allegation in order to get you removed from the murder investigation, the explanation must be that he saw you as a danger to his liberty. And the only way in which you could be such a danger would be if you had some vital piece of evidence in your possession."

"But I haven't!"

"Not consciously perhaps."

"It's about the craziest theory I've ever heard. It's based on an entirely false premise, namely that I know something damaging to him. I don't. Your theory as good as supports his allegation that I told him I was in possession of a vital piece of evidence against him which I'd suppress if he gave me a bribe."

This had, indeed, occurred to Clare and it was only her conviction of her husband's innocence that had caused her to think along other lines. As it was she had to admit that Paul Frensham had shown considerable boldness in making the particular allegation if her theory were, in fact, correct.

On the other hand, if she was right in her reconstruction and if Frensham had urgently needed to have Nick taken off the murder enquiry, the only way he could achieve this was to make an accusation of serious impropriety, which postulated an allegation of corruption. And if that was the case, the form of allegation virtually wrote itself.

"Humour me and play along with my theory a bit further, whatever you may think of it," she said with an affectionate squeeze of his hand. "Accept that you did see or hear something without realising its significance, and try and think back to when you were at the Frenshams' house. The odds are it was something in his bedroom. You searched it and, apart from the sweater, you didn't find anything you regarded as important, but what was there in the room? Think terribly hard, Nick."

"Clothes," he said in an uninterested tone. "There were clothes lying all over the place, he was obviously pretty untidy."

"Only *his* clothes as far as you recollect?"

"Yes. I don't remember seeing any female garments if that's what you mean."

"Anything that might be associated with Mrs. Isaacs?"

"No-o, not that I recall."

"Close your eyes and put yourself back in Paul Frensham's bedroom. Did you see any money lying around?"

"No. I particularly searched for money. He had three or four pounds in his wallet and that was all."

"You'd have noticed, wouldn't you, if he'd had any female jewelry in his bedroom?"

"I hope so," Nick said with a faint grin. "The nearest approach to jewelry was a small red button thing on his dressing table."

"Why do you say button *thing*?"

"It looked like a large piece of candy. Simon would have had it in his mouth in no time at all. I only noticed it because of its bright colour. But it certainly didn't wink at me and say, 'I'm a clue.' "

"Where exactly was the sweater?" Clare asked with a frown.

"Hanging over the back of a chair against a radiator. I could see it was wet before I touched it. I asked him if he'd been wearing it the previous afternoon at Mrs. Isaacs' and he said he had—I suppose he thought we could find out anyway and therefore he'd better tell the truth—and I asked him why it had just been washed and he said because he'd got mud on it from Mrs. Isaacs' garden. He certainly became agitated when I said I was going to take possession of it. He even tried to seize it from me."

"Will the lab have reported yet?"

"Pitcher may have had a preliminary report on the phone about some of the stuff that was submitted, but I doubt even that."

"If they can find traces of the deceased's blood on the sweater, that'd be enough to charge Frensham with the murder, wouldn't it?"

"Provided it's not also his own blood group."

For a time both of them just stared ahead occupied with their own thoughts.

When Nick spoke, it was as though he were voicing the conclusion of a long line of silent thought.

"Even if Frensham is charged, it doesn't get me off the hook." With a note of bitterness he went on, "In fact, he's more likely to stick by his allegation if he finds himself in the dock. It'll form part of his defence. I'll be dangled in front of the jury as the real villain of the piece." He paused. "And worse still it'll hold up Upperton's inquiry. Section forty-nine investigations are invariably shunted into a siding until the complainant's trial is over."

"That doesn't have to be, does it?" Clare asked in a worried tone.

"It usually is the form, unless the complainant, who is also a defendant, makes a great fuss and provided there won't be a clash of interests."

"I can't see Sir Guy Frensham wanting the investigation into his son's complaint held up. Not that he's going to get any joy out of the result in any case."

"So we hope."

"He can't," Clare said firmly. "The sole evidence in support of the allegation is his son's word. There can't be any corroboration because it doesn't contain any detail to corroborate. It's word against word which, at worst, leaves the charge non proven."

"Is that meant to be comforting?" Nick asked in a spiky tone.

Clare sighed. There were going to be many such moments and she must resist the impulse to snap back.

It was, however, unfortunately true that even if Paul Frensham was charged with murder, it would do nothing to resolve Nick's situation.

The trouble was she was unable to see any way by which she could keep in touch with the murder enquiry. She didn't know any of the officers involved for the simple reason that Nick had been on loan to the division in question to help them cope at a time of overwork and worse than usual under-manning in the C.I.D. She felt that this last fact had increased his feeling of gall. It was as though battle reinforcements had succumbed to sickness as soon as they reached the fighting zone.

As if to make up for his petulant outburst, he now suddenly asked, "How was Helen?"

"Who?" Clare's mind was a thousand miles away from the small deception she had conceived earlier in the day.

"Helen, your cousin!"

"Oh . . . oh, she was fine. Sent you her love." Jumping up from the sofa, she said, "I'll start getting supper."

She had suddenly felt she had to get out of the room before the depression which had swept over her became apparent. The euphoria induced by her meeting with Alice M. Macpherson had evaporated in the face of Nick's own mood.

Her efforts seemed to have landed her in an abrupt dead-end. And not only landed her in one, but would keep her there unless she could think of some further initiative which was open to her to take.

There just *had* to be something more she could do. She realised how important it had suddenly become for her own morale. It wasn't enough merely to sustain Nick on the domestic scene, all her instincts as an ex-detective constable cried out for militant action on his behalf.

Action which would help to dissolve the great black cloud which hung over him and threatened to engulf them both.

Chapter 8

"If you'll just wait in here, I'm sure Mr. Rooke will be free in a few minutes."

The middle-aged female, who had ushered him in, retired, leaving Oliver Gill alone in the waiting-room. On a low table in the centre of the room were a number of legal periodicals as though to encourage clients to brush up the law on their particular problems while they waited to be seen. Oliver Gill chose the only alternative which was a copy of the previous day's *Times*. But after a brief glance at the front page, he dropped it back on the table and went and sat down on one of the chairs which were set against the wall.

He wondered whether Mervyn Rooke really was engaged in another matter or whether it was simply a psychological gimmick to keep his clients waiting for a statutory period.

He had known Rooke for about ten years and though each of them would probably refer to the other as a friend, they were in truth no more than acquaintances. On the rare occasions that Gill wanted legal advice, he always came to Rooke and Co. Mervyn Rooke had until recently been the firm's sole principal, but a few months ago he had taken in a junior partner whose name appeared below his own on the official note-paper.

The door opened and the same middle-aged female appeared.

"Mr. Rooke will see you now if you'll come this way."

Gill followed her down a short corridor. She knocked on a door at the end and stood aside for him to enter.

"Hello, Oliver; not seen you for quite a time. Hope the world's been treating you well."

Rooke was short and rotund with a bald head that made him look older than his actual years. He came round his desk and shook Gill warmly by the hand.

"Take a pew and tell me what brings you thirsting after the law."

As Gill sank into the depths of the visitor's chair, Rooke sat back in his desk chair and swivelled it round so that he looked straight down on the other man.

"You know that my aunt died recently?" Gill said.

"No, I didn't know that. Sorry to hear it. She was your only relative if I remember correctly? Died suddenly, did she?"

"Very. She was murdered."

"Oh, good gracious me. What a terrible shock for you! Ought I to have read about it in the papers?"

"Her name was Florence Isaacs. She lived at Finchley. She was murdered just under a week ago."

"If I did read of it, I'm afraid it didn't make any impression. The newspapers these days are so full of violent happenings that one's eye tends to glide quickly over them." He did a rapid swivel to the left and back again. "Have the police made an arrest yet?"

Gill shook his head. "I think they suspect a seventeen-year-old youth who used to do odd-job gardening for my aunt. He was there on the afternoon in question. I imagine they're making sure of the evidence before they arrest him. They've probably got to be a bit careful as he's the son of Sir Guy Frensham."

"What! That old T.V. phony?"

"He's also an ex-M.P."

"And isn't he always reminding us of the fact!" Rooke had another quick swivel before returning his gaze to his visitor. "Anyway, to business. Am I right in surmising that you have come to see me about your aunt's will?"

"Yes."

"Inherited the bulk of her estate, have you?"

"One hundred pounds to be precise."

58

Mervyn Rooke's jaw dropped and for a second his chair became motionless. "Oh, dear! Who's she left it all to?"

"A number of charities. They'll benefit to the tune of eighty or ninety thousand pounds when the estate's settled up."

"And you only receive a hundred pounds? Did it come as a bit of a shock?"

"I certainly expected more than that. I thought she'd leave me several thousand at the very least; perhaps even the bulk of her estate." He paused and passed his tongue nervously over his lips. "That's what I've come to see you about, Mervyn. I'd like to contest the will."

"I'm sure you would, Oliver, but one has to have grounds."

"Doesn't the fact that I'm her sole surviving relative count for something?"

"Absolutely nothing. You were only her nephew and she wasn't obliged by law to leave you even a paltry hundred pounds."

"What sort of grounds were you referring to just now?"

"That the will was not a valid will because, for example, she was not of sound mind when she executed it."

"What would the effect of that be?"

"If a court declared against the will, the effect would be that she died intestate."

"Then as her sole surviving relative, everything would come to me, wouldn't it?"

"In theory, yes. But it would depend on a whole lot of unknown factors such as the circumstances in which she came to make the will and had there been a previous will and if so what were its terms? Don't raise your hopes, Oliver. The fact that your aunt treated you despicably is not evidence of unsoundness of mind. It's extremely unlikely that the charities concerned would let go without a fight and indeed the executors would probably feel bound to oppose any attempt to upset the will. Incidentally who are the executors?"

"Her bank."

"Couldn't be worse. Banks are quite flintlike in these matters. Sentiment doesn't enter into their calculations. Self-interest is their only guiding principle. I expect she's left the manager of her branch a legacy?"

"Five hundred pounds, I'm told."

"Bank managers get quite a nice additional income from the bequests of grateful old ladies." He swivelled slowly away from Gill and then swung back again. "When was the will made?"

"About a year before her death. I'd like you to find out about any previous wills. Can you do that?"

"Probably. Do I take it, Oliver, that you wish to instruct me officially in the matter?"

"Yes, if it won't be too expensive."

"It shouldn't be. But I ought to repeat that I don't think you're going to get any joy at the end of it all."

"Supposing a later will came to light?" Gill asked in a guarded tone, as though hand-picking his words.

"Yes?" Rooke remarked with a note of suspicion.

"Well, supposing it did?"

"If you suddenly turned up flourishing a later will which purported to leave everything to you and which you said you'd found hidden in a drawer beneath your aunt's underwear . . ." Rooke threw out his arms in a gesture of mock surrender. "Well, you'd have a fair amount of explaining to do."

"Because they'd jump to the conclusion that it had been forged?"

"The possibility would certainly be looked into, shall we say."

"Supposing I'd been her son, instead of her nephew, would that make any difference?"

"Not in law. If you read the papers you'll know that a parent frequently disinherits a son or a daughter. Generally speaking, a testator can leave what he likes where he likes. Not that he's likely to have very much to leave these days. The exchequer sees to that." Another quick swivel and he sprang from the chair. "It's been nice seeing you again, Oliver, though I'm sorry I can't give you more cheerful tidings. I'll find out what I can about your aunt's will." He pushed a pad of paper across the desk. "Just write down her full name and the name and address of her bank."

They shook hands at the door, which Rooke closed almost abruptly, leaving Gill to find his own way out of the office.

On returning to his desk, Mervyn Rooke sat down and gave himself a couple of three-sixty degree turns in his chair.

I really believe he'd have gone away and embarked upon a bit of forgery if I'd given him any encouragement, he reflected. I hope he doesn't get up to any foolishness. I've always thought he was something of a grasshopper. I wonder why his old aunt treated him in such a derisory manner.

Oliver Gill, for his part, walked away from the solicitor's office in a mood of dejection. Mervyn Rooke had succeeded in dashing all his hopes and had left him reflecting once more how monstrously unfair life was. The only thing was that, this time, the feeling was reinforced by a more than usually active resentment of his plight. He gave a vicious kick at a small pebble on the pavement and watched it ricochet off a wall and strike the ankle of a girl standing in a bus queue. The girl turned and glared at everyone in the vicinity. Gill just stared back, experiencing a temporary relief. She shouldn't have been standing there, anyway. Moreover, she had a disagreeable expression, so it served her right.

Chapter 9

One thing Detective Chief Inspector Pitcher felt quite certain about was that Rivings would seek to get in touch with Paul Frensham as a result of the police visitation. Pitcher reckoned that a meeting would be fixed, that it was likely to be as soon as possible and, as a long shot, that there was a good chance of it taking place at Jox's Disco which was their regular rendez-vous.

Accordingly, on the evening after Pitcher and Lyle had called at the Rivings home, Detective Constable Bax found himself at Jox's accompanied by Woman Police Constable Sanderford. Each of them was appropriately dressed for the occasion, Bax in a skin tight shirt open to his navel and a pair of frayed and faded jeans and W.P.C. Sanderford in a long dress which gave the appearance of having been worn day and night for several weeks.

They sat sipping Coke and trying to look as bored as the dozen or so other young people who were present.

"I hope we get some action," W.P.C. Sanderford said quietly without a change of expression.

"The guvnor sees it as a longish gamble," Bax replied. "If neither has turned up by midnight, we'll quit."

It wasn't long after that, however, when Bax gave his partner a sudden ankle tap beneath the table. "Here's one of them now! He's coming this way, so don't look round."

A moment later Paul Frensham passed by their table and, as providence would have it, sat down at the next one.

He was frowning hard and looked anxious. He immediately lighted a cigarette and stared about him with a quickly assumed air of boredom.

It had been arranged that given the opportunity, Bax should maintain a watching role while W.P.C. Sanderford, whose hearing was as acute as a sheep-dog's, should get as close as possible, even though it meant having her back to them.

In pursuance of this plan, she excused herself and departed for the ladies cloakroom. While she was away, Bax got up casually from his seat, had a stretch and sat down in the one she had vacated from where he could observe Frensham.

Tony Rivings arrived at the same moment as W.P.C. Sanderford returned to the table. He walked briskly across to where Frensham was sitting. He was glowering and failed to respond to the nervous little smile with which he was greeted. He sat down and pulled his chair closer to the table in a meaningful way.

"What've you been telling the law about me?" he asked in an aggressive tone.

"Nothing, Tony," Frensham said, with a vehement shake of his head.

"You gave them my address?"

"No, I didn't. I promise you I didn't."

"How'd they know about you and me then?"

"Search me." Frensham's tone was placatory.

"If it weren't you, it must have been your father—or that iceberg who pretends to be a girl. It can't have been anyone else."

"I'm sure Kersty wouldn't have given them your name."

"That leaves your father. If you'll excuse my crude language, he's a s.o.b. your father."

Frensham gave his companion a sickly smile. "All fathers are at times."

"Yours more than most. What's he trying to do, get me picked up so that the heat's taken off you? You better tell him that I'm no one's fall guy and if he tries anything funny in that line, it'll be his own precious son who finds himself pushed off the ladder. Got the message, Paul?" Frensham managed to give a small nod while nervously biting his lip. "Good, then we understand each other and can move on to the next item on the agenda, as they say." He glanced round the now crowded basement room with its wall posters and hideous lighting. "Let's get out of this dump and go some place we can talk nice and quiet." He rose. "I think the guy at the next table's planning to rape you from the look on his face."

With an enormous effort at self-control, Bax contrived not to react to this outrageous observation, which he surmised he'd been intended to overhear. W.P.C. Sanderford, however, shot him an apprehensive glance. He even refrained from looking up as they passed the table on their way out.

W.P.C. Sanderford made as if to move, but Bax motioned her to stay seated. "We can't follow them after that. It'd be too obvious." He paused. "And I don't mean rape!"

Pitcher was still in his office when they returned to the station. He listened to their account with a quietly attentive air.

"I'm glad my hunch paid off," he said when they had finished. "I wonder what else they wanted to talk about? If we get enough to charge Frensham, we might be able to frighten Rivings into telling us much more of what he knows." He paused with a thoughtful expression. "We might yet try doing that anyway."

Chapter 10

As soon as he arrived in his office the next morning, Pitcher put a call through to the laboratory. He was anxious to find out the results of any preliminary tests, though he knew it would be some time before he received a comprehensive report. But even evidence based on a preliminary test could be sufficient to found a charge.

He found himself speaking to a Detective Sergeant Ingram, one of the laboratory's liaison officers whose function it was to protect the scientific officers from constant interruption.

"Hold on, sir, and I'll find out what's happened so far. I know Mr. Broughton was working on some of the material yesterday evening." It was several minutes before Sgt. Ingram returned to the telephone and he sounded out of breath. "Sorry I've been so long. Mr. Broughton's gone straight to court this morning and I couldn't find his notes, but I have them now." Pitcher could hear the crackle of paper as Ingram sorted what he had brought back. "Deceased's name, Florence Isaacs, is that right?"

"Correct."

"Sample of deceased's blood group AB," he read. "Bloodstains on deceased's clothing all group AB. Ditto sample of blood taken from bedroom carpet. Cast iron mould depicting King Charles spaniel heavily stained at head end with group AB blood." He paused. "In fact, all the blood stains are of that group. Doesn't help you very much, I suppose?"

"Not really. What about a man's brown sweater? Has that been examined yet?"

"Hold on, I think there's something about that on the next sheet. Yes, here we are. It had been recently washed in an extra strong solution of detergent. There was evidence of staining on the front of the right sleeve about an inch up from the cuff. It could have been blood. Further tests may determine this but it's unlikely that it'll prove possible to group it. Is that better news?"

"Much."

"Now wait a moment, there's something else here if I can decipher Mr. Broughton's note. Item S.B. thirty four, one green earring. Spots of blood of group AB on front and on clasp at rear. Wool fibers entwined in clasp similar to fibres in composition of brown sweater. That sounds more interesting, doesn't it?"

"It's the best news yet," Pitcher said with a note of restrained excitement. "The sweater belongs to our prime suspect so that bit of evidence puts him fairly and squarely at the scene of the murder. Can I take it as quite definite?"

"Well, I wouldn't want you to rush off and arrest him without confirmation from Mr. Broughton, but that's what his note says. It could be that Mr. Broughton has further tests in mind." There was a renewed rustling of paper. "Incidentally, we seem to have had only one green earring. Is that right, sir?"

"Yes. We only found one. It was on the floor close to the body."

"Perhaps she was a bit mad and only wore one. Presumably it came off when your suspect was attacking her. Anyway, sir, that seems to be all I can tell you at the moment. I'll have a word with Mr. Broughton when he returns from court."

For a while after he had rung off, Pitcher stared across the room deep in thought. Then he reached for the phone once more and dialled the number of the Director of Public Prosecutions Department.

"I wonder if I might come and see you later to-day, sir," he said on being put through to one of the Assistant Directors whom he had met on a number of previous occasions. "It's a murder enquiry . . . No, you haven't had a file yet . . . I'm wondering if I've got enough to prefer a charge . . . Half-past two will be fine, sir . . ."

Mr. Neve, the Assistant Director, whom Detective Chief Inspector Pitcher visited that afternoon, had the appearance of a relaxed, even lazy, man, which, in his case, was not deceptive, as he was both these things. But after thirty years in the D.P.P.'s office he had acquired a sensitive nose for trouble and a shrewd ability in avoiding it. Allied to a reasonable degree of common sense, these instincts enabled him to occupy a hot seat with a minimum of traumas.

In a large room overlooking the park, he greeted Pitcher affably and waved him to a choice of chairs.

"What's the trouble?" he asked when they were both seated.

"I don't know whether you've read anything about the case, sir. There's been quite a bit in the papers."

"If I have, I'm afraid none of it has stuck. Tell me what I need to know."

For the next few minutes, Pitcher outlined the facts while the Assistant Director listened in silence.

"Are there any other suspects apart from the Frensham boy?" Neve asked at the end.

Pitcher frowned and shifted his position in the chair. "I don't know that you'd call them suspects, sir. There's this man Unsworth, whom we've been unable to trace, who left the deceased's house after a mysterious row about a fortnight before her death. We'd certainly like to find him and discover what the row was about, but we don't have any evidence to link him with the murder. Then there's Gill, the deceased's nephew. He doesn't appear to have been on very friendly terms with his aunt and she left him only a hundred pounds in her will, but, again, there's nothing to link *him* with the murder."

"Did he know he was getting only a hundred pounds?"

"No, it appears to have come as a rude shock."

Neve nodded thoughtfully. "Whereas against Frensham you have opportunity and some scientific evidence which puts him at the scene. What about motive in his case?"

"My guess, sir, is that he went into the house to do a bit of thieving and killed Mrs. Isaacs when she caught him at it."

Neve made a slight face. "Rather over-reacting wasn't he, if that's the way it was? After all, at worst he only stood to be given the sack."

"She might have threatened to call the police. And one also has to remember, sir, that he'd want to avoid any public scandal for his father's sake."

"Perhaps . . . Anyway, motive's not an element the prosecution have to prove, though it's always reassuring to find one."

"Oh, I'm sure we shall find one all right, sir, once we've charged him."

"And that's what you now want to do?"

"If you think the evidence is sufficient?"

"I think you're almost there but not quite, particularly bearing in mind that it's Sir Guy Frensham's son." Quickly Neve went on, "I'm not suggesting that different rules apply in his case, but first I think one wants to be quite sure before one charges any seventeen-year-old with murder and, secondly, one has probably got to be prepared for Sir Guy to react vigorously. He's likely to thrash out like a harpooned shark. And that's an additional reason for making sure of one's ground before launching out." He leaned forward and straightened the leatherbound blotting pad on his desk while Pitcher waited for him to go on. "On the other hand, I can see every reason why you should interview him again and invite him to explain how fibres from his sweater came to be adhering to an earring found beside the murdered woman's body." He paused and added with a smile, "I can tell from your expression that you're not exactly enamoured of the idea."

"Any further interviews with Frensham will have to be conducted in the presence of a solicitor and I was hoping to avoid having to see him again." Pitcher's tone was resigned.

"I can understand how you feel, but I think you must see him. I think he's not only entitled to be given an opportunity of explaining the matter, but you'd also be protecting yourself against possible later criticism." Neve stared hard out of the window for a few seconds, before turning back to face his visitor. "For example, we know that Frensham was legitimately at the house that afternoon. Supposing Mrs. Isaacs called him in and asked him to do something to the clasp on her earring, bend it, tighten it, loosen it, anything. In doing so, he could have held it against his sweater . . . You'd look pretty silly if you rushed in and charged him with murder; and then that came out and away goes your vital piece of evidence down the plughole. On the other hand if he has no plausible explanation to offer or even any explanation at all, that particular piece of evidence is considerably strengthened."

Pitcher nodded slowly. "If I must see him, I must. Supposing, sir, he doesn't have any explanation to give, do you think I have enough to charge him?"

"Just about, bearing in mind also the freshly washed sweater, concerning which he has clearly been evasive. If the lab can confirm that there was blood staining on it, Frensham will either have to deny it or explain it. He's told you that the washing took place because it was routinely dirty. If the lab can prove blood on it, he'll have to change his story or say they're wrong. Assuming they're not wrong, you'll just have another small nail in his coffin."

"I'd better make arrangements to see him as soon as possible," Pitcher said, squaring his shoulders.

"Give me a call afterwards and let me know what transpired," Neve said amiably. "I'll be happy to advise you any time. It certainly sounds as if Frensham's your man and, as I said a few minutes ago, I think you've almost got enough. It mayn't be the strongest of cases, but there'll be something for him to answer and even a reasonable prospect of a conviction at the end. Scientific evidence, if it sticks, is probably the best one can get these days. Fibres and flakes of paint found in awkward places—awkward from the defendant's point of view, that is—can be much more effective than evidence of the defendant exclaiming 'it's a fair cop, guv.' "

"They actually do say that quite often," Pitcher remarked with a grin. "It's almost embarrassing as no one ever believes it's true."

"The trouble is 'verbals' have become so discredited that juries just won't accept them any longer, unless they're corroborated in some way." Neve was about to get up but sat back in his chair. "Incidentally, you mentioned that Frensham had made an allegation of attempted bribery against one of your officers, is that being investigated contemporaneously?"

"Yes, sir. Detective Chief Superintendent Upperton of A.10 is in charge of the enquiry."

"Oh, they've given it to the professor, have they? I can't see him standing any nonsense from Sir Guy Frensham."

"The officer concerned, Detective Sergeant Attwell, has been suspended pending the outcome."

"I imagine that was done for reasons of tact," Neve remarked. Noticing Pitcher's expression, he went on, "I can read your thoughts, Mr. Pitcher. He wouldn't have been suspended if it hadn't been for Sir Guy in the background. I'm afraid we have to accept that there are double standards in these matters. It's hypocritical to pretend otherwise. But if not suspending him meant a great public furore created by Frensham senior, it seems to me reasonable that he should have been suspended because such a furore would probably cause far greater harm to the image of the police than suspension will to the unfortunate Sergeant Attwell."

"It's all politics," Pitcher said bleakly.

"Of course it is. Politics of one sort or another dominate all our lives all the time. Though this is more a question of expediency. But not even Sir Guy Frensham can get Attwell dismissed without evidence, any more than he can prevent his son being charged with murder if the evidence does exist. So when it comes down to basics, we still do live by the rule of law—despite police disillusionment on the subject. Anyway, I gather you're satisfied that Frensham's allegation against Attwell is groundless?"

"Completely."

"Which means presumably that it was made as a sort of smoke-screen to cover—what?"

Pitcher shook his head. "I'd like to know."

"I'm sure you will before the end," Neve said in an encouraging tone.

When he arrived back at the station, Pitcher found a message from Sergeant Ingram of the laboratory. It said that he had spoken to Mr. Broughton who was ready to swear that the woollen fibres found attached to the earring were not merely similar but identical to those from which the sweater was woven. He would also testify that the staining on the sleeve of the sweater was from blood, but due to the vigorous washing he was unable to say whether human or from an animal.

Pitcher read the message a second time with increased satisfaction. Feeling fortified, he went up to his office and immediately dialled the Frensham's number. Kerstin Borg answered.

"I'd like to speak to Sir Guy Frensham."

"Who is it please?" she asked in a polite but impersonal tone.

"Detective Chief Inspector Pitcher."

It was several seconds before she said, "I will see if he is here."

A silence followed and then Pitcher heard a door being slammed and a moment later the receiver came to life.

"Sir Guy Frensham speaking." The voice was coldly formal.

"This is Detective Chief Inspector Pitcher. I'm in charge of the enquiries into Mrs. Isaacs' death. I'd like to interview your son on one or two points."

"What points?"

"I'm not prepared to discuss them on the phone, Sir Guy."

"I shall require any interview to be held at my solicitor's office."
Pitcher smothered the mild obscenity which begged to be uttered.

"Certainly, but I'd like to arrange the interview as soon as possible.
Sometime tomorrow for preference."

"I can't see why you're in such a hurry," Sir Guy remarked
sharply.

"Because I'm investigating a murder and public opinion expects us
to get on and not waste time. I seem to recall, Sir Guy, hearing you
once castigate the police for dilatoriness, so I'm sure you'll understand the situation."

"I'll see what I can arrange," Sir Guy Frensham said in a tone
festooned with icicles.

"Who is your solicitor?" Pitcher enquired.

"Mr. Woodside of Hillary, Woodside and Hastings. They have
offices in Montague Square."

Pitcher jotted down the name and address for checking in the Law
List. He had no doubt, however, that it was a firm of the utmost
respectability. Probably never came closer to crime than when one of
their clients shot the traffic lights at red.

"If you can call me back within the next hour, I'd be grateful," he
said.

"I'll do my best," Sir Guy replied in a surprisingly amenable tone.
"I'm sure you'll appreciate, Chief Inspector, that I have no wish to be
obstructive. On the contrary, there is no more staunch supporter of
the police than myself. As you will know if you have watched any of
my programmes, I'm a law and order man. I'm always exhorting the
public to regard the police as friends. On the other hand I've never
shrunk from pointing out any rotten apples in the barrel. I realise
that my son Paul may be in possession of evidence which can assist
your investigation, but you must remember that he's only seventeen
and that he's still considerably shaken as a result of his experience with
your Sergeant Attwell. That's why I'm sure it's in everyone's interest
that any further interviews should be held in the presence of my solicitor who can advise Paul as we go along." He paused. "And, of course,
I shall be present myself."

Pitcher had an uneasy feeling after ringing off that the forthcoming
interview was destined to produce some nasty surprises for one side
or the other.

He hoped that he was going to be entirely at the giving end.

His suspended sergeant had been on his mind the past couple of days and he decided that he would call him now.

Nick himself answered the phone and immediately recognised the voice at the other end.

"I thought I'd just phone and find out how you were," Pitcher said in a tone of slight embarrassment.

"Bored and fidgety, but otherwise all right, sir," Nick replied in a voice which betrayed his own feeling of awkwardness. "How's the enquiry going? Or perhaps I shouldn't ask that."

"I don't see why not and I don't see why I shouldn't answer either. It's beginning to look more and more as if young F. is our man. The lab has come up with some helpful bits and I'm hoping to interview our young friend tomorrow. Unfortunately his father insists that it must be in the presence of the family solicitor."

"I suppose that was to be expected, sir."

"I'd like to think that something may emerge which'll assist you, Nick."

"So would I, but I can't see it happening. I was saying to my wife that the deeper he finds himself involved, the more he's likely to cling to his allegation."

"I'm afraid that may be so. Though I still can't conceive of your being in any danger from his allegation."

"I've been suspended, sir, and I can assure you it's no fun. If anyone believes it's just a holiday, let them wait until it happens to them."

"I'm sorry, Nick, I know how sore you must feel. I was only trying to convey that the allegation can never be proved, so it's bound to be all right in the end. It's worth hanging on to that, whatever your feelings at the moment."

"I'm afraid I'm apt to fly off the hook a bit these days. I haven't yet adjusted to my present status. I didn't mean to jump down your throat."

"Forget it! I realise what an ordeal it must be and I just hope it won't be too protracted."

"Thanks, sir. What about the rest of the enquiry? Any sign of Unsworth yet?"

"No. We traced him so far, but then he disappeared from sight. I reckon his row with the deceased is no more than a red herring, but we've got to find him in order to eliminate him."

"And the nephew?"

"I didn't much care for him, but that doesn't make him a murderer.

And obviously his aunt didn't care for him either. She left him a paltry hundred pounds."

"If you can find out, sir, why our young friend made that allegation against me, I'm sure you'll be three quarters on the way to proving your case." Nick's voice carried a note of pleading.

"Don't worry, I'm very conscious of the position. Just cross your fingers for me when I see him tomorrow."

"I'll certainly do that. And thanks for ringing, sir, I appreciate it."

As Nick dropped the receiver back, he couldn't help reflecting that there was Pitcher only two years older than himself and a detective chief inspector, and here was he a detective sergeant, suspended.

It was the suspension part that he really felt. To be the subject of a complaint and of an enquiry by A.10 was the lot of a great many officers these days, but only a small minority were actually suspended from duty pending the outcome. Suspension was a cruel humiliation which would leave its scar even if he were to be reinstated with crowds waving and bands playing.

He stood for a moment at the bottom of the stairs, but no sound came from Simon's room.

He wished that Clare hadn't gone out. This sudden rush to see relatives and friends she'd not visited for ages was all very fine for her, but she appeared to ignore how he felt being left so much on his own. He realised it was part of her plan to force him to look after Simon, but she was carrying her therapy to a callous length.

He glanced at his watch. It would be at least three hours before she was back.

A wife's place at such a time was at her husband's side. The more Nick reflected on it, the sorrier he felt for himself. It would serve her right, if she arrived home and found him dead.

At this more melodramatic thought, he gave a rueful shrug. Yes, all right, he was brimming over wtih self pity. But how was he expected to react? As if he were just waiting his turn to have his hair cut?

Chapter 11

It was with a sense of desperation more than hope that had taken Clare on a personal reconnaissance of the area in which it had all happened. It was, she reasoned, the only thing open to her. To go and look at the Frensham house and afterwards at 14 Teeling Road. The odds were that any eventual gain would prove to be more useful to a house agent than to the wife of a suspended police officer who was trying to clear her husband's name.

She felt that it would somehow be a plus if she so much as managed to catch a glimpse of Paul Frensham. She could then at least believe that her journey hadn't been as pointless and futile as a small voice kept telling her it was likely to be.

She had no difficulty in finding the Frenshams' house. She had looked up the address in the telephone directory and then studied a street map so that she would not have to ask for directions when she arrived in the neighborhood.

The first time she walked past, she noticed two cars in the drive, but no sign of life within. She continued for fifty yards, then crossed to the other side of the road and made her way back at a more leisurely pace.

The Frensham scene appeared precisely the same as it had four minutes earlier. What had she expected, she asked herself bruisingly? She could hardly go on patrolling indefinitely up and down without drawing attention to herself. It was patently a rich area and therefore one that would be burglar conscious.

At this point she noticed that the house diagonally across from the Frenshams had a "For Sale" board outside. A quick look told her that it was already empty and so she shot through the gate and slid behind a privet hedge.

Satisfied that her furtive move had not been observed, she got herself in a position from where she could see the front of the Frenshams' house, but was herself concealed from view.

For fifteen minutes nothing happened and she felt overwhelmed by a sense of futility. It was one thing to do this on instructions as a serving policewoman—and she often had; but to do it on one's own initiative and with no other idea in mind, save that in some obscure and roundabout way it might help Nick, did seem the height of futility.

She had just decided that she would stay a further five minutes when she saw the front door of the Frenshams' house open and a tall blonde girl emerge.

Clare's heart gave a small hopeful leap. It must be Kersty.

On reaching the pavement Kersty turned left and walked away from where Clare was keeping watch.

Clare gave her twenty yards and then slipped from her hiding place and set off along the opposite pavement.

The Swedish girl moved with the litheness and coordination of a natural athlete and Clare was obliged to quicken her pace in order not to lose distance.

About two hundred yards along, Kersty crossed diagonally to Clare's side of the road and vanished round a turning to the right.

Putting on further speed, Clare reached the turning and then only just avoided colliding with Kersty who was on her way back. As it was she had to step to one side, though Kersty paid her scant attention.

A few yards down the road to the right was a familiar red letterbox, its presence at once explaining the Swedish girl's expedition.

For a couple of minutes, Clare leaned against a wall while she regained her composure. Physical exertion plus the sudden excitement had left her out of breath and she could hear her heart drumming away.

By the time she retraced her own steps, darkness had fallen and there were lights on in the Frenshams' house, but the downstairs curtains had been drawn so that she was unable to see into any of the rooms.

Ten minutes later she was back at the bus stop. Should she or should she not make her way to Teeling Road? All she was likely to see was the black hulk of an empty Victorian house.

On the other hand, it wouldn't take long to get there and, after all, she was in the area.

In the event, the decisive factor was the fillip to her morale at seeing Kerstin Borg. If she had come away, so to speak, empty-handed from the first part of the evening's enterprise, she'd probably have gone straight home. She might even have done so, had she known what a tiresome journey it was going to be, involving a bus change with a long wait.

Teeling Road, when she found it, was tree-lined and ill-lit. Several of the houses appeared to be in complete darkness and those that were showing any light did so with modesty, if not downright parsimony. It was very different from the opulent ambience of where the Frenshams lived.

If Clare had been of a nervous disposition, she doubted whether she would have taken her quest any further. There was something distinctly spooky about the road after dark, especially when a soft wind brought the trees to life and their branches cast darting shadows around the intermittent street lamps. Luckily, there was one such lamp opposite number 14 so that Clare was able to discern the figures 1-4 painted on the stucco-ed pillar of the front gate.

The three storey house lay twenty yards back from the road. There was a small half crescent of drive bounded by laurel bushes. From where she stood at the front gate the drive appeared to be pitted with holes.

14 Teeling Road, scene of the murder of Mrs. Florence Isaacs, widow aged 63. Fancy living there alone, Clare reflected as these details passed through her mind.

Suddenly, her whole body stiffened. She was sure that a torch had been shone in an upstairs window. But it hadn't been for more than a second. It was as though someone had used a torch for a quick look into the room.

It was while she was trying to make up her mind what to do that she became aware of approaching footsteps along the pavement. She stepped hurriedly inside the gate and slipped behind one of the laurel bushes until whoever it was had passed.

To her astonishment, the person turned in and moved stealthily along the edge of the drive. She saw a figure reach the front door before merging into the background darkness.

There was a faint metallic scratching noise, followed by a rusty squeak and a quiet click.

Someone had opened the front door and gone in. The sounds had been unmistakable. Moreover, it was someone with a key.

Crouched in her hiding-place Clare strained her ears. A couple of minutes or so after the man had entered she thought she heard distant indeterminate noises from within the house, but it could have been her imagination. Her heart was beating so furiously it would have been difficult to hear external sounds of less than explosive magnitude. As she kept her gaze riveted on the front of the house, her eyes began to see strange coloured spots floating in their vicinity. She closed them for a time and tried to concentrate on her next move, though she already knew she must stay until something further had happened. There could be no question of creeping away and tamely catching a bus home at this crucial juncture.

She reckoned she'd been there about ten minutes when she heard a sudden sound of movement at the side of the house. The next thing was that someone moving at great speed dashed past her laurel bush and out of the gate.

She had the firm impression that it was not the person who had entered through the front door, though there had been no question of seeing his face or identifying any item of clothing. It was an impression based on movement more than anything.

If she was right, then clearly the man with the key was still inside the house. She would give him five minutes to emerge before deciding what to do. It was also conceivable that the other person would return, though that seemed unlikely from the haste of his departure.

When five minutes was up, Clare crept from the cover of the laurel bush and cautiously approached the house. On reaching the front door, she tried the handle; but to no avail. The catch must have been slipped when he entered. She could see it was a Yale lock.

Then recalling that the departing intruder had come from the side of the house, she decided to reconnoitre round the back.

It didn't take her long to find the scullery window which had obviously been forced and which was now flapping in the wind.

She clambered through, thankful that she was wearing trousers, and then paused to wipe off any fingerprints she might have left.

It seemed a wise precaution, as she had no idea how the evening was going to end. It seemed unlikely that she would be invoking the aid of the police and, on the other hand, she didn't wish to complicate their task if and when their attentions were directed to the scene.

It was only as she finished her cleaning operation that it occurred to her that she had probably removed other prints apart from her own. Well, it was too late now and. . . . she gave a shrug, she hoped it didn't matter, but if it did, that was just too bad.

She stood in the middle of the scullery for a few minutes waiting for her eyes to become accustomed to the darkness inside. She could see the door which led into the kitchen and a cold, sour smell of stale cooking assailed her nose.

On the further side of the kitchen was the outline of another open door and a moment later she found herself in the hall with the front door to her left.

She had always prided herself on her ability to move quietly in the dark and felt stimulated by the challenge of her present circumstances.

At the foot of the stairs, she paused and listened intently. Suddenly the pervading silence was fractured by a groan from somewhere above. Clare stifled a gasp of fear and tensed herself. A second later there was a faint thump as though something had been dropped on a carpeted floor. This was followed by a further and louder groan.

One thing for sure, there was nothing to be gained by standing in a dither where she was. She either went upstairs and explored or she got out quickly.

On reaching the landing at the top of the stairs, she could see that only one door was open. She tiptoed across and paused on the threshold when something knocked against her leg. She jumped back as though she had trodden on a snake and peered anxiously down at a shape on the floor.

Cautiously, she knelt beside it and put out a tentative hand. The sound of heavy breathing told her what she had already guessed.

Her hand touched the man's face and he let out another groan.

"I'll get you some water," Clare whispered.

The time for ultra caution had passed and she felt along the wall until she found a light switch. The landing light, which had an ancient tasselled shade, gave forth a dim and yellow reflection.

Clare found the bathroom at the second door she opened and returned with a plastic beaker of water.

The man was lying as she had found him with his eyes still closed. She held the beaker to his lips. Most of the water ran down the side of his chin, but some went into his mouth.

His eyes flickered open and his expression became startled as he stared uncomprehendingly at Clare.

"Where am I?" he said in a hoarse whisper.

"You're in Mrs. Isaacs' house. You remember Mrs. Isaacs?"

The eyes which had been looking at Clare in an unfocussed sort of way became suddenly suspicious.

"Who are you?" he asked, raising his head but letting it fall back again with a wince of pain.

"Just say I'm the neighbourhood Good Samaritan," Clare replied, running her hand gently round the back of his head. She could feel a bruise the size of a pigeon's egg behind his right ear and he let out a small cry of pain as she touched it. "Somebody belted you one. Do you know who it was?"

He shook his head painfully. "I don't remember anything."

"Not even letting yourself in through the front door with a key?"

"Yes."

"Whoever it was must have been waiting for you up here. Does that make sense?"

"Who are you?" he asked again in a puzzled tone.

Clare could see that their dialogue was in danger of becoming a series of unanswered questions unless something was done to steer it determinedly on to a more profitable course.

"I'm a private enquiry agent," she said with some truth and then added with rather less, "we're working for the executors of Mrs. Isaacs' will."

The man frowned as though trying to slot this piece of information into his existing knowledge.

"For the bank?" he said in a worried tone.

Clare nodded, unaware until then that the bank were the executors.

"But what are you doing here? I don't understand. . . ."

"Let's just say that I was sent to keep an eye on the house. And it's as well for you that I was," she went on quickly, deciding to make capital out of her ministering angel role. "If I'd not come in and found you, you might have died."

The man frowned again in an obvious effort to focus his muzzy thoughts.

"My head hurts," he said, and closed his eyes.

Clare extracted a soiled handkerchief from his breast pocket, poured water over it from the beaker and held it against the bruise behind his ear.

"Would you like me to call a doctor?" she asked, fairly certain of the answer she would receive.

"No, no doctor."

"Or the police?"

This time he put out a hand and clutched her arm—as though to prevent her translating words into action.

"No, no one."

"I shall have to inform my employers, of course."

His grip on her arm tightened.

"No." He turned his head painfully and looked at her. "Please, no."

"I can only help you if you tell me who you are," Clare said, having been maneuvering toward this point.

"I am no one. It doesn't matter."

"Don't be silly, of course I must know who you are. After all, it's a serious matter breaking into a murder victim's house. If the police were to find out. . . ."

"No, no. The police mustn't know." He raised himself up and then clutching hold of the end of the bed managed to clamber to his feet. "Oh, God, my head!" he groaned.

But Clare was in no mood to give sympathy unless it served her purpose.

"I know who you are," she said. "You're Derek Unsworth."

From the outset she had decided that he must be either Mrs. Isaacs' nephew or Unsworth. And of the two, it seemed to her that only Unsworth would be so anxious not to be involved with the police. After all, it couldn't be for nothing that he had disappeared and eluded their efforts to find him.

"How do you know who I am?" he asked with an anguished gasp.

"Much more important is, what were you doing here, Mr. Unsworth?"

He swayed slightly and closed his eyes. "I can't remember . . . . anything."

"In the first place," Clare went on, "you had no right to keep the door key when you left. The fact that you did so indicates you intended coming back. What brought you back tonight?"

"I can't remember."

Clare shrugged. "If you won't tell me, then it'll have to be the police."

"Somebody hit me as I came through the door."

"We know that. This is Mrs. Isaacs' bedroom, isn't it? What did you come back to look for?"

"I want to be sick," he said, in a tone of urgency.

Clare stood aside to let him pass on his way to the bathroom, but he was hardly through the door when he made a sudden dash downstairs. Clare reached the top of the staircase in time to see the front door slam behind him. The noise reverberated through the empty house like a cannonade.

"Damn!" she exclaimed vigorously. She returned to Mrs. Isaacs' bedroom and gazed round its shadowy interior which was lit only by the dim glow of the landing light.

On an impulse, she walked across the room and drew the heavy curtains over the windows. Then she switched on the bedroom light.

Two other people had come looking for something that night, why shouldn't she make the third? The only difference was that presumably the first two knew for what they were looking, whereas she had no idea.

As soon as she had turned on the light she noticed that most of the drawers were open. It appeared that someone had had a quick and not too untidy rummage through the contents. The impression was of a more considerate customs official who had been searching for contraband.

This must have been the first intruder as Unsworth had obviously been assaulted and rendered unconscious as soon as he entered the room. Clare conjectured that they had not both been looking for the same thing. She might be wrong about this, but she thought probably not. In any event, what interested her most was Unsworth's quest. What could have brought him back to the house? He clearly wasn't any ordinary burglar, which the first man might well have been. He had come back to look for something specific. Something, moreover, which he expected to find in the murdered woman's bedroom.

Unsworth, who had lived in the house and got on famously with Mrs. Isaacs until they'd had their mysterious row which had resulted in his abrupt departure. Unsworth, who had taken a door key with him, for which the only explanation was that he expected to return. Unsworth, who had returned on a dark night a week after the old lady's violent death. Unsworth, who had obstinately eluded the police and had now slipped off Clare's hook.

These were the thoughts which ran through her mind as she made her own cautious search of the bedroom. But she found nothing which might have any bearing on the crime or have excited the acquisitive instincts of anyone other than the most indiscriminating scavenger.

She found herself staring at the dark stain on the carpet at the foot of the bed. A small square in the middle had been cut out and the whole area of stain had been outlined in chalk. There were other small chalk circles which the laboratory scientist had made wherever he had found blood spots.

She stepped round these and was about to switch off the light and draw back the curtains when her eye was caught by something sticking out beneath the bedspread close to where Unsworth had been lying. It was a piece of paper and she bent down to pick it up. It was the somewhat crumpled, torn-off flap of an envelope.

On it was written an address, 28 Malabar Road, S.E.11. It had clearly fallen from Unsworth's pocket, possibly when she extracted his handkerchief.

It was with a feeling of considerable satisfaction that she placed it carefully in her own pocket.

Half way downstairs a sudden thought jolted her mind. All the time she'd been presuming that Unsworth had come to look for something.

But supposing he had come to *leave* something?

Clare hardly noticed the tedious journey home with its changes by bus and tube. Moreover, she felt fully capable of handling Nick whatever mood she found him in.

She became aware of the man sitting opposite her staring at her in an interested way and realised that her expression had probably been reflecting her thoughts, which at that moment had been centred on Nick's reaction if she told him how she had spent her evening.

She unfolded her evening paper and pretended to read. Suddenly her eye did focus on a short item under the "Home News in Brief" heading. It read: "Scotland Yard to-day confirmed that a detective sergeant has been suspended in connection with an allegation of corruption made by Sir Guy Frensham, the well-known T.V. personality. It is understood that an investigation is under way."

It could only have been Sir Guy Frensham himself who had leaked the information to the press, Clare reflected bitterly. And now they'd be delving to discover the name of the officer and Nick could expect to be hounded by phone calls.

For one savage moment, Clare wished she'd thrown a bomb at the Frensham house, instead of merely staring at it.

Chapter 12

At ten minutes to four the next afternoon, Detective Chief Inspector Pitcher and Detective Sergeant Lyle presented themselves at the office of Messrs. Hillary, Woodside and Hastings in Montague Square.

There was a uniformed commissionaire at the entrance and an extremely attractive girl at a large oak desk in one corner of the vestibule.

Pitcher gave her their names and she consulted a typed list.

"Yes, you are expected, Mr. Pitcher," she said unsmilingly. "If you'll just take a seat in the waiting-room."

She led them down a passage and flung open a door, closing it with a firm click once they were inside.

Sergeant Lyle gazed round the room.

"Doesn't live up to the entrance—or the receptionist," he remarked, wrinkling his nose.

"This is probably the second-class waiting-room," Pitcher replied.

"You don't think Sir Guy and his like are put in here then?"

"They'll be in the V.I.P. room. Free gin and leather-bound copies of Halsbury's statutes round the walls."

"Is that the sort of firm it is?"

"They've got a fair number of showbiz clients, I gather. Also a sprinkling of belted earls. I made a few enquiries of a solicitor friend of mine, that's how I know."

"They certainly seem a bit different from the ones who ply their trade in the local magistrates' court," Lyle said, still looking around him. "So much as mention the word 'rape' in this office and they'd probably turn the fire extinguisher on you."

"After first rescuing your cheque book," Pitcher added, with a wry smile.

Somewhere in the distance, a clock struck four and Pitcher checked his watch. At a quarter past, he got up from his chair and paced restlessly round the room.

"I'll give someone just five more minutes," he said grimly. "If nobody's come to fetch us by then, we'll start to make a fuss. And I mean *a fuss*."

"It's a bit of psychological warfare, sir, keeping us waiting like this."

"I know it is and it's rotten psychology at that."

It was almost, however, as if their conversation had been overheard for a minute later the door opened and a grey-haired female with spectacles said, "Come this way please," and stalked off along the passage, leaving them to gather up hats and coats and hurry after her.

A small lift took them up one floor and they stepped out into an atmosphere of executive opulence. Not only were the carpets thicker but the various fittings also reflected a no-expense-spared attitude.

This was the partners' floor and whatever dramas might be enacted in their respective offices, nothing was allowed to seep through the walls.

They passed out of a small lobby and through swing doors which hissed as they closed behind them. The grey-haired woman knocked discreetly on the last door on the left and then held it open for Pitcher and Lyle to enter.

It was a large light room with windows on two sides and Mr. Woodside's green leather topped desk set at an angle between them. Mr. Woodside himself was standing in the middle of the room as though on cue. He was a short, slightly podgy man whose obviously expensive clothes looked rather a waste of money on him. Pitcher put him in his late thirties.

"Come in, gentlemen," he said. Making a sweeping motion with his arm, he went on, "No need for introductions as you know one another."

Sir Guy Frensham and his son were sitting over at a table. Sir Guy gave the officers a formal nod, but Paul, who wore an expression of pouting boredom, disdained to look up.

"I suggest you two gentlemen sit opposite my client and I'll take the umpire's chair at the head of the table." He gave a short barking laugh and sat down. "Before we begin, perhaps we ought to establish a few rules. I understand you wish to ask Paul some questions in connection with your enquiry into some old lady's death. . . ."

"Her murder actually," Pitcher remarked.

Mr. Woodside frowned. "As I was saying, in connection with your enquiry into an old lady's death. Obviously if there is any assistance my client can properly give, he will do so, though from what I know I think it is most unlikely that he can help you any further. I shall, of course, advise him on the propriety of your questions and at this point I ought to mention that the interview will be recorded." He threw Pitcher an uncompromising look. "No objections, I take it, Chief Inspector?"

"None. Do you intend to supply the police with a copy of the tape?"

"That's something we can discuss later," the solicitor said quickly. Then in a blander tone he went on, "Now, I've cleared the air, perhaps we can begin. Chief Inspector?"

Pitcher's first reaction to Mr. Woodside had been anything but favourable. The solicitor might have a comfortably podgy look and a quite genial expression, but inside was someone who clearly regarded chief inspectors as upstarts who must be kept in their place, particularly when they entertained thoughts of harassing the son of one of his important clients.

He took his eyes off the solicitor who was sitting back in his chair with a look of quiet superiority and glanced across at Paul who still wore a sulky air but seemed a trifle nervous. Near to him sat Sir Guy Frensham, chin rested on knuckled hand in a pose known well to his viewers on T.V.

Focusing his gaze on Paul, Pitcher said, "I want to ask you some questions about the sweater you handed to the police. . . ."

"Tch! I'd like it clear on the record that my client did not hand the sweater to the police, it was seized by Detective Sergeant Attwell without right or justification."

"Shall I go on?" Pitcher asked quietly.

"Yes, provided you don't misrepresent the facts."

"The laboratory tells us that there is evidence of blood-staining on the sweater. Can you explain how it got there in the first place?"

"What sort of blood-staining?" Mr. Woodside asked, sharply.

"The laboratory is unable to say. . . ."

"Well, really!"

"Because the sweater had been extra thoroughly washed shortly before it came into the possession of the police."

"I must have rubbed up against something," Paul said in a mumble.

"Can you remember doing so?"

"No."

"When did you first notice the blood?"

"I've not said I ever noticed it. The sweater was washed because it was filthy. I didn't know anything about any bloodstains on it. That is, if there were any," he added on a note of defiance.

"One moment, chief inspector," Mr. Woodside broke in. "May I ask the purport of these questions?"

"To establish how your client's sweater became blood-stained."

"Am I to understand that you are questioning my client as a suspect?" the solicitor enquired in a tone of incipient outrage. "Because, if so, you ought to know that it's your duty to caution him."

"If I decide it's necessary to caution him, I shall do so at the proper time, which is when I've made up my mind to charge him. I haven't yet reached that stage and probably never will if Paul can satisfactorily explain how his sweater became blood-stained."

"Your tone is verging on the offensive," Mr. Woodside remarked.

"I'm sorry, but it's very difficult to conduct an interview against running interruptions."

"I hope you're not trying to tell me my job, chief inspector."

"I wouldn't dream of it, any more than you'd try and tell me mine."

It was Sir Guy who now spoke. "Our cat is always becoming involved in fights with others in the neighbourhood and as she makes a bee-line for Paul's lap when he's around, he could quite easily have got some of its blood on him." He turned toward his son. "That's so, isn't it, Paul?"

"Yes, that must be it," Paul said with obvious relief.

While the bloody solicitor and I squabble like two kids, bloody Sir Guy thinks up the answers, Pitcher reflected savagely. Well, he won't find it so easy next time round.

"There's a further point about your sweater that invites an explanation," he observed, outwardly equable. "Some fibres from it were found adhering to a green earring which was discovered on the floor close to the dead woman's body."

"Whose earring?" Mr. Woodside demanded. He glanced at Paul. "You don't wear earrings do you?"

Paul coloured and shook his head. "Of course not," he mumbled.

Pitcher couldn't fail to notice Sir Guy's expression which had become a mixture of puzzlement and vaguely distant comprehension.

"We don't know whose earring," Pitcher said in a careful tone. "But what interests us is how fibres from Paul's sweater became adhered to it and how the earring came to be at the scene of the murder? I'm sure you'll all agree that both points are of some significance?"

"Is this the lab again?" the solicitor asked querulously.

"Yes, as a result of tests, that's their conclusion."

"I'd like to know what tests?" Sir Guy said angrily. "I happen to be aware as a result of a programme I presented that a lot of so-called scientific evidence is no sounder than a witch doctor's remedy for a brain tumour. If you expect an answer to your question, the best you can do is satisfy us that you're asking it from a sound premise. That is, if you can."

Sir Guy might be looking angry, but his son was constantly moistening his lips, which had suddenly acquired the dried, greasy appearance of one in the grip of fear. Pitcher noticed with interest the change of mood which had overcome him.

"I'll explain as best I can," he said in a tone of quiet confidence. "The fibres taken from the earring together with sample fibres from Paul's sweater have been examined under a low power microscope, first in a white light and then in ultra violet light which causes fluorescence and enables a further comparison to be made. Finally both lots of fibres were subjected to thin layer chromotography which separates a dye into its component colours. As a result of all those tests the scientific officer who carried them out is quite positive that the fibres found adhering to the earring came from the sweater."

"Where'd you get the sweater?" Sir Guy asked almost aggressively, turning on his son. "It was Marks and Spencer's, wasn't it?" he went on, without waiting for an answer.

Paul swallowed hard and nodded immediately.

Sir Guy swung his attention back to Pitcher. "There must be tens of thousands of sweaters of that colour in circulation? These fibres you talk about could have come from any one of them."

Pitcher shook his head. "Not if you accept the lab evidence."

"We don't accept it for one moment," Mr. Woodside broke in.

"I'm not quite sure where all this is supposed to be leading us, but if you're intending to make some sort of issue out of it, then of course we shall want our own expert to examine the fibres." He paused and glared at Pitcher. "Perhaps you'd say exactly what you are getting at?"

"I'd like to know if Paul can offer any explanation?"

The solicitor began to speak but Sir Guy rode over him. "Why my son should be expected to explain how fibres similar to those from his sweater came to be attached to an earring which came from you know not where, save that you accept my son doesn't himself wear earrings, is beyond any reasonable explanation."

"Quite so," Mr. Woodside remarked contemptuously.

"May I take it that is also Paul's answer?" Pitcher asked.

"His answer," the solicitor said, "is that, on my advice, he doesn't feel obliged to comment on these so-called findings by the laboratory."

"Is that right, Paul?" Pitcher asked. The boy's waxy pallor had become even more noticeable in the last few minutes and he did no more than give a nervous nod, as his father cast him another covert glance in which doubt and speculation were mixed.

"It will not have escaped your notice, chief inspector," Mr. Woodside said with a portentous frown, "that this sweater of Paul's was seized by the officer who subsequently solicited a bribe from him. I don't know whether it was the same officer who conveniently found the earring at the scene? But it seems to me a matter of some significance and one which you or the other investigating officer should look into."

"Are you suggesting that police planted this evidence?"

Mr. Woodside shrugged. "I'm doing no more than pointing out a rather curious coincidence."

"I think that's all as far as I'm concerned," Pitcher said after a pause, pushing back his chair. "Unless there's anything further Paul wishes to say?"

"My client has nothing further to say. He came to this interview in good faith and feels that you have attempted to take advantage of him by unfair questions. Unfair because they were not questions he could possibly answer at this stage. Nevertheless, he utterly repudiates their accusatory import."

Realising that the solicitor's rhetoric had been directed at the tape recorder, Pitcher decided not to give him or it the satisfaction of any reply.

Mr. Woodside accompanied the officers out of the room, murmuring, "I'll be back in a moment," to Sir Guy Frensham. In the corridor, he said, in a worried tone, "Between ourselves, chief inspector, are you considering a charge against Paul?"

"That's for others to decide. I shall merely report on the result of the interview."

"Who will decide?"

"I shall be making my report to the D.P.P."

"Oh!" Mr. Woodside seemed nonplussed. "Paul's a rather shy, perhaps somewhat spoilt, boy, but I hope he didn't give any impression of being obstructive. It's just his manner, which is a bit unfortunate."

"What are you worrying about?" Pitcher said with a sudden quick smile. "You've got a fully taped record of everything that passed. Why not play it back and see if *you* think he was being obstructive?"

On their way back to the station in the car, Sergeant Lyle said, "I reckon we've got enough to charge him."

"I'd still like to clear up the mystery of that green earring," Pitcher remarked in a thoughtful tone. "Where'd it come from?"

"It can only have been the deceased's and it must have come off when she grappled with Frensham."

"If that's so, where's its twin? She certainly wasn't wearing it and we've not found it among her possessions. So where was it?"

"We'll find out sooner or later, sir," Lyle said.

"It'd better be sooner." He frowned in concentrated thought. "One green earring could wreck our case against Paul Frensham unless we can account for it."

Chapter 13

"I don't think it's an awfully good idea, letting him play with those. He could swallow one."

As soon as she had spoken, Clare regretted her tone which had been sharper than she'd intended.

She had looked through the sitting-room door on her way upstairs to see Nick hidden behind a newspaper and Simon sitting on the floor playing intently with a pile of coloured counters.

"He likes them and they keep him quiet," Nick retorted, lowering his paper for a moment to look at his son. "You're not to put them into your mouth, Simon, do you hear, it worries your mother."

Clare bit her lip. It would only need one further incautious comment from her to fuel a row. Nick's own tone made this clear. It said, in effect, you've given me the role of nanny so now keep out of the nursery.

Perhaps it had been a mistake after all to make him take charge of Simon, but something had had to be done to fill the acute vacuum in his life and what else? Simon, at least, didn't seem to have any complaint.

90

"He's just put one in his mouth," Clare said and shot away upstairs. Almost immediately she heard a wail of frustration as the counter was rescued.

It was a few minutes later while she was making their bed that she heard her name being shouted.

"Clare! Clare!"

"I knew it," she said to herself as she dashed out of the bedroom, "now he's swallowed one."

But when she got downstairs, it was to find Nick kneeling on the floor beside Simon holding a counter between forefinger and thumb of each hand. One green and one red.

"Earrings," he said excitedly. "Would it be possible to have a pair of earrings of different colour."

"I've never seen any," Clare said, "but that doesn't mean they don't exist. Sort of fun earrings, you mean? But what are you getting at, Nick?"

"Don't you remember my telling you we found a green earring at the scene of the murder? Actually, it was not unlike a slightly padded counter and it was watching Simon playing with them that made me think of it."

"And?" Clare said, with a puzzled expression.

Nick was looking at her hopefully.

"There was that red button thing I noticed in Paul Frensham's room," he explained, his eyes shining eagerly. "It could have been the twin of the green earring."

"Kersty Borg's," Clare exclaimed, infected by Nick's excitement. "We must find out if she had such a pair. I'll . . . why don't you call that girl you met, Alice Macpherson?" She had prevented herself just in time from giving away the fact that she'd met Alice.

"Yes. Of course I could just pass the suggestion to Mr. Pitcher and let him follow it up, but it'd be much nicer to give it to him gift-wrapped."

Clare nodded eagerly. "Call her now, Nick."

While he was dialling the number, she gazed speculatively at Simon who was happily scattering the counters as widely as he could. He glanced up and gave his mother a look which seemed to invite her co-operation in furthering the chaos on the floor.

"Hello, is that Miss Macpherson?" Nick said. "This is Nick Attwell speaking. You may remember me . . . ? Oh, good. . . ." He gave a shy laugh. "Yes, I suppose it was a fairly memorable meeting in the circumstances. I'll tell you why I'm phoning. It's about the Frensham's au pair girl, Kerstin Borg, do you happen to remember whether she ever wore earrings? . . . Oh! Yes, it is rather a curious question, but the answer could be important. . . . You could? That'd be terribly kind of you. . . . Well, as soon as possible . . . my wife?" He gave Clare a faintly surprised glance over the top of the phone. "She's fine. . . . Well, if you can call back soon, that'll be great. One of us will be here. Yes, she does know who you are."

Nick replaced the receiver. "She's going to phone her friend who knows Kersty Borg and ask her. She says she doesn't recall whether or not she was wearing earrings on the few occasions they met." He smiled at Clare. "You'd like Alice."

Clare returned his smile. "That's a reckless thing to say to one woman about another." She knelt down beside Simon and began picking up counters. "But you could be right in this case."

"She enquired after you almost as if she knew you," Nick added.

Clare made no reply and was able to hide her expression by diving under the table to reach for a far-flung counter.

In under twenty minutes Alice Macpherson had called back to say that yes, Kersty was apparently given to wearing rather way-out earrings. In answer to a question from Nick, she was able to confirm that the Swedish girl did, indeed, have a pair of different colours. What Alice's friend had described as her port and starboard pair.

It was with a profusion of gratitude that Nick rang off. Then stepping over Simon, he threw his arms around Clare and kissed her enthusiastically.

"You were right all the time, darling. It must have been because Frensham was sure I'd noticed the red earring in his bedroom that he made his allegation against me. He assumed I'd put two and two together, but I never did until now. And only now thanks to Simon playing with those counters."

"It looks as if Kersty Borg may have been concerned in the murder," Clare remarked.

"That figures. She and Paul could have been in it together. She appears to have had him under her thumb, thanks to his complete infatuation with her."

Clare let out a happy sigh. She just prayed that Nick's euphoria was not going to prove short-lived. It was wonderful to see his spirits raised off ground-level for the first time since his suspension.

"What are you proposing to do now?" she asked.

"Phone Mr. Pitcher and tell him about the earrings. Then let Chief Superintendent Upperton know as well."

"How are you going to explain your knowledge of Kersty's earrings without bringing in Alice Macpherson?"

"I hadn't thought of that."

"And not so much her as her friend."

"Mmmm. What do you suggest?"

"I think you'd better call her and explain the situation. There's no reason to think her friend won't be willing to make a statement to the police if necessary, but it's only fair to warn her."

"I'll do that. Though for a start I can just tell Pitcher that's my information. His first move will be to tax them with it. It'll only be if the Borg girl denies ever having had such a pair of earrings that Alice's friend's evidence will become important."

"That's true," Clare said. "I'll remove Simon while you make the call."

Pitcher listened to Nick without comment until the end. Then he said, "That's likely to be my best bit of news today. I reckon we'll be feeling Master Frensham's collar before the sun goes down." And he proceeded to give Nick a résumé of the laboratory evidence and of his interview in the solicitor's office the previous afternoon. "I only said to Reg Lyle last night that the mystery of one green earring could wreck our case against Frensham, but now the mystery's been solved." He paused. "Well, partially solved."

"Why only partially, sir?" Nick asked, in the tone of one who suddenly saw a prize being snatched from his grasp.

"What was Frensham doing with one of his girl-friend's earrings at the scene of the crime?"

"But it had fibres from his sweater adhering to it," Nick said, as though this explained everything.

"Yes, indeed," he said thoughtfully, and went on, "I'd like to think the red earring still exists, but I fear that's a remote hope."

"So do I, sir. They'll have destroyed it as soon as Frensham got back from the police station, but it explains his allegation against me."

"Do you want me to speak to the professor or are you going to tell him yourself?"

"I thought I'd call him, sir. If I can't speak to him, I'll try and get Sergeant Young."

"Good. Meanwhile, I must decide just how to tackle this. It seems to me your information postulates two solutions. Either Paul Frensham had his girl-friend's green earring pinned to his sweater when he was at Mrs. Isaacs' house that afternoon—*or* his girl-friend went to the house wearing *his* sweater, which in these unisex days is quite possible." He paused. "I wonder if that's what actually happened. While he was working in the garden, she was up to no good in the house?"

The sunshine of a mellow October afternoon was able to ameliorate the pervading darkness of Malabar Road, S.E.11, but only fractionally.

When Clare arrived outside number 28, she noticed the sign in the front window which said "vacancies." After ringing the bell and waiting some time, the door was opened by an elderly woman with straggling grey hair.

"I'm looking for Mr. Unsworth," Clare said, with an encouraging smile.

"There's nobody of that name lives here," the woman replied.

"He's a young man with fair, wavy hair brushed back and a thin face."

"Sounds like Mr. Worth," she said, giving Clare a dubious look. There was something in her tone which suggested that lodgers with false names were not unknown to her. "He's not in, either."

"When does he usually arrive back?"

"He's only been here a few days. He might be back around half-past five. It might be later. I don't clock them in and out. As long as they pay their rent and don't make a nuisance of themselves, they comes and goes as they chooses."

"Do you happen to know where Mr. Worth works?"

"Couldn't tell you. None of my business where he works."

"Thank you," Clare said with a disarming smile. "I'll probably call back later."

"Suit yourself," the woman said, indifferently.

It was only five o'clock and Clare had told Nick that she'd be home around seven. He had accepted this without comment, being still buoyed up by the morning's events. She had noticed a café on the corner of Malabar Road and the main road and decided to go in there and have a cup of tea.

While she drank her tea, she tried to decide whether or not the time had come to reveal to Nick what she had been up to. If she did, he was bound to discourage her from pursuing her private enquiries, particularly if she told him of the escapade at Mrs. Isaacs' house two nights previously and this seemed reason enough not to make any premature disclosure to him. Sooner or later, she would, of course, have to tell him but, meanwhile, she decided to maintain her deception.

She had just steered herself toward this conclusion when she heard the door of the café open and looked up to see Unsworth come in.

He went up to the counter and ordered a poached egg on toast and a cup of tea. Unaware of her presence, he went and sat at a corner table and began reading the evening paper.

Clare waited until he had been served before carrying her own cup of tea over to where he was sitting.

"May I join you?" she said, at the same time taking the chair opposite him.

He stared at her with a suspicious, yet puzzled, expression.

"Perhaps you don't remember me?" she went on.

"I think you must be mistaking me for someone else," he said in a wary tone.

"We met at Mrs. Isaacs' house, two nights ago. How's your head?"

If Clare had ever wished to see someone jump out of their skin, this was as near as she was ever likely to get to the phenomenon.

"Who are you?" he asked fiercely.

"If you're wanting to know how I found you, the answer is that a piece of paper with your address in Malabar Road dropped from your pocket. I found it on Mrs. Isaacs' bedroom floor after you'd made your precipitate departure. As to who I am, I told you that last time we met. I'm a private enquiry agent."

"What do you want with me?" he asked, glancing about him nervously.

"I hope you're not thinking of making a dash for it again," Clare said, "because if you do, I shall definitely set the police on to you. And I have the impression that's something you wish to avoid at all costs. Your only alternative is to talk to me and this seems as good a place as any."

He was staring at Clare as though mesmerised by her presence, while his poached egg slowly congealed on its thinly buttered piece of toast.

"Let's start with recent events and work back," Clare went on. "What I'd like to know first is what you were doing in Mrs. Isaacs' house the night before last?"

Chapter 14

At about the same time that Clare was starting her inquisition of Derek Unsworth, Detective Chief Inspector Pitcher and Detective Sergeant Lyle were making their way to Heathrow airport with as much speed as the rush-hour traffic permitted.

It had been a day of frustration since Nick's telephone call. First Pitcher had been unable to get any reply at the Frensham house when he rang and this state of affairs had continued until the middle of the afternoon when at last somebody answered. It turned out to be Lady Frensham who sounded on the phone as colourless and negative as the wife of Sir Guy probably had to be if they were to live in peace under the same roof.

In reply to Pitcher's request, she informed him that Kerstin Borg was at that moment on her way to the airport where she was due to catch an early evening plane to Stockholm.

This piece of information had come in nervous fragments as though she feared that just talking to the police might be regarded as a form of high treason.

Realising this Pitcher had not prolonged their conversation, but had immediately put a call through to the Special Branch police at the airport.

The result had been that, as soon as she had passed through Immigration Control, Kersty was taken aside and politely asked to accompany a young plain-clothes officer to a sparsely furnished room along a short corridor of anonymous doors.

It was there that Pitcher and Lyle found her about half an hour later. Pitcher at once noticed with quiet satisfaction that the experience had obviously unnerved her, which was all to the good, so far as he was concerned. It meant that the softening-up process was already under way.

"You have no right to stop me," she said, springing up from her chair as soon as they entered.

Pitcher motioned her to sit down again. "Just keep calm, Miss Borg, and with luck you'll still catch your plane or certainly the one after."

"What is it you want?"

"Why are you returning to Sweden?"

"It is my holiday."

"May I see your ticket?"

Frowning, she opened her bag and produced it. "You see, it is in order."

"I also see that it was purchased today," Pitcher remarked. "Rather a sudden holiday, isn't it?"

She gave an impatient shrug. "I do not have to answer your questions, I think."

"You do if you want to fly to Stockholm today—or even tomorrow. Tell me, was it Sir Guy Frensham who suggested you should take this holiday?"

"It is not wrong to take a holiday, I think."

"Just answer my question."

"Sir Guy thought I should have a holiday," she said sullenly.

"When did he suggest it?"

"It was last night perhaps."

"Did he tell you it would be a good thing if you left the country for a time?"

"He said I should go on my holiday," she said, glancing nervously at the floor.

"Did he tell you why?"

"I do not know anything about it."

"About what?"

"About all that has happened. It is not nice for me."

"What isn't?"

"All this trouble with his son."

Pitcher nodded. "We seem to be making some headway at last. What do you know about Paul and Mrs. Isaacs' death?"

"Nothing, nothing," she exclaimed in a tone of alarm.

"What do you know about a pair of earrings, one red and the other green?"

A hand flew up to her mouth as though jerked by a string as she let out a small gasp. She shook her head dumbly.

"Look, Kersty," Pitcher said in a not unkind voice, "I'm not trying to scare you but I must know the truth. An old woman has been brutally murdered and it's your duty to assist in any way you can. I don't care what Sir Guy Frensham has told you to the contrary, your job is to answer my questions truthfully. It's quite clear that he was trying to bundle you out of the country before we could talk to you again and it's equally clear why he was doing so: to protect his son, Paul. That's right, isn't it?"

The girl's cool, disdainful air had long since vanished and now nervousness and worry were written all over her face.

"Look, I'll strike a bargain with you," Pitcher went on in a tone of quiet persuasion. "Once I'm satisfied that you had no part in the murder and that you've told me everything you know, I'll guarantee you a place on the next plane to Sweden."

"I did not murder the old woman," she said desperately. "You must believe me. Please believe me."

"Have you ever worn Paul's brown sweater?"

Her expression changed immediately to one of surprise. "No, I never wear it."

Pitcher let out a silent sigh of relief. Her expression more than her words told him that she was speaking the truth and this removed the restraint he'd felt under so long as she might turn out to be implicated in the crime.

"Tell me about the earrings." Pitcher said.

"I bought them in Copenhagen at one of those shops where they sell sex jokes."

Pitcher blinked. "In what way are they sexy?" he enquired on a note of interest.

"If you show your boy friend the green one, it means he may come on."

"What, jump into bed with you?"

"It is only a joke."

"And if you blink the red one at him, that means nothing doing, I suppose?"

"Yes," she said with a small wan smile.

"Just like traffic lights," Sergeant Lyle observed.

"And how did Paul come to have the green one?"

"I give it to him."

"As a permanent come hither?"

"Please, I do not understand."

"It doesn't matter. And where's the red one?"

"I threw it at him when I am angry."

"When was this?"

"After he tell me that he has lost the green one and he thinks it must be at Mrs. Isaacs' house."

"That's what Paul told you, is it?"

"Yes."

"And it was that which made you angry?"

"I tell him it is stupid of him. Sometimes he is like a little boy." Her tone held a sudden note of scorn.

"Were you in love with Paul?"

"No, I just let him sleep in my bed. He thinks he was in love with me, but he had never been in bed with a girl before, so how can he know?"

"He was infatuated with you?"

"Infatuated? What is infatuated?"

"Passionate about you."

"Yes, he is always wanting sex with me."

"Did Paul tell you what happened at Mrs. Isaacs' house that afternoon?"

"He is very frightened. He comes home and says he has found her murdered. He has blood on his sweater and I wash it for him."

"Did he tell his father this?"

"No. He only tell me. And I am cross with him because he could get me into trouble by losing the earring."

"How much does Sir Guy know about all this?"

"I think he guess that Paul is in trouble."

"Why did Paul say that Sergeant Attwell tried to obtain a bribe from him?"

"I don't know."

"Surely Paul has discussed it with you?"

"No. Perhaps it is true."

Pitcher frowned. Why was she suddenly being evasive?

"Are you sure you don't know?"

She nodded vigorously. "After it happened, I am angry with Paul and we are cool together."

"But you washed his sweater for him."

"That is before he tells me everything. Then I am angry with him."

"How long are you going to stay in Sweden?"

"Sir Guy says he will tell me when to come back. But I think, perhaps, I do not return," she added.

"Supposing you are needed as a witness, will you come back if asked?"

She searched Pitcher's face as if to find the right answer to his question.

"If you ask me, I come."

"It might mean giving evidence against Paul; would you still come?"

"Paul and I are finished," she said in a tone that even sent a small chill through Pitcher.

"All right," he said after a pause, "we'll just get you to sign a statement and then you can get your plane—or the next one that's going. But you must promise to return if we need you as a witness."

"I promise," she replied, but in a tone so glib that Pitcher knew he was giving a hostage to fortune in letting her go. On the other hand, he had no power to keep her in the country and if she did fail to come back when asked, he would meet that difficulty at the due time.

Later, as they drove away from the airport, Sergeant Lyle suddenly said, "Do you know what I'd like more than anything else, sir? To see Sir Guy Frensham in the dock charged with obstructing the police, trying to impede a prosecution and attempting to pervert the course of justice."

"Nothing else?" Pitcher enquired, in a note of irony.

"Aiding and abetting murder?"

"How do you work that one out?"

"Procreating the little so-and-so who did it."

Chapter 15

As soon as he reached his office the next morning, Pitcher put through a call to Mr. Neve, the Assistant Director of Public Prosecutions with whom he'd had earlier dealings and asked if he might come and see him as soon as possible.

"Any time that suits you," Mr. Neve replied amiably. "I shall be in all the morning."

Pitcher had scarcely replaced the receiver when his phone rang and the officer on the switchboard told him that a Mr. Oliver Gill wished to speak to him.

"Do you want him put through, guv'nor?"

Pitcher hesitated a second before agreeing. "All right, I'll take it."

"Oliver Gill here," said a voice that Pitcher recognised. "I thought I'd give you a ring to find out how your enquiries are going?"

"They're proceeding, Mr. Gill."

"No arrest yet?"

"Not yet."

"Any prospect of one, do you think?"

"Like the Mounties, we always hope to get our man."

Gill give a small, unamused laugh. "I'm only asking because I still hope to contest my aunt's will and it'll help me when I can point out that someone's actually been charged with her murder."

"Oh!" Pitcher didn't see how, but was not sufficiently interested to pursue the point.

"I suppose you haven't come across a will in the course of your searches at the house?"

"No. Anyway, I understood that her will was lodged at the bank."

"It is. Or, at least, the bank hold the one of which they propose to obtain probate. But it's dated a year before her death and I still have a feeling that she might have made another and kept it in the house."

Pitcher found himself frowning. "One leaving the bulk of her estate to you, do you mean?"

"I'm afraid that's too much to hope. However many wills you might find, my expectations would remain at zero."

"Then what makes you think there may be other wills?"

"She was one of those professional will makers. Quite frankly, I thought she might have made a fresh one after Unsworth entered her life. Incidentally, have you managed to trace him yet?"

"No, he's not come forward and we've no idea where he is."

"Funny the way he's disappeared. I suppose it's possible he mayn't know of my aunt's death or that you've been looking for him?"

"If he's gone abroad, it's quite possible."

"Have you found any clue as to what it was he rowed with my aunt about?"

"No. But from all you've told me about her, she wasn't the easiest person to get on with. A row could have blown up out of almost anything."

"I'm afraid that's true. She could be a difficult old lady. That's why she had no friends to speak of. She was at best on terms of armed neutrality with many of her neighbours and Mrs. Rawlings only continued working for her because she was a bit odd herself. Before her, daily women came and went as though they were on a conveyor belt. They just wouldn't put up with her ways and I can't say I blame them. As I've told you, it was only family feeling that made me visit her."

"Yes, I recall your telling me that," Pitcher remarked drily. In fact, he didn't for one moment believe that Gill would have gone on visiting his aunt if he'd known that there was only £100 for him at the end. He now went on, "Mr. Gill, I have to go out in a minute, so if there's nothing further you have to say, I'll ring off."

"It's just that I thought I ought to keep in touch with you. I'll continue to do so if I may. After all, I am your victim's only surviving relative."

If also a disinherited one, Pitcher thought. For some reason of his own, Gill was clearly interested in the outcome of the police investigation. Whatever that reason was, Pitcher was sure it had little to do with a nephew's affectionate memory of his deceased aunt.

Ten minutes later he and Detective Sergeant Lyle were on their way to Queen Anne's Gate where the D.P.P.'s department was situated.

Mr. Neve received them with his usual affability.

"The reason for this visit, sir," Pitcher said, "is to tell you the result of our further interview with Paul Frensham and of some fresh information we've had from Kerstin Borg, the Swedish au pair girl."

Mr. Neve listened in silence while Pitcher, with an occasional chip-in from Lyle, brought him up to date with the enquiries. At the end he said, "Well, you've certainly got a stronger case than you had previously. With Kerstin Borg's evidence, I consider that you now have enough to charge him. But is she going to come back when we want her?"

Pitcher shrugged, but Sergeant Lyle nodded encouragingly.

"Why are you so sure?" Neve asked with a sceptical grin, looking in Lyle's direction.

"I just think she will, sir. She was being honest with us and I don't think she'll let us down."

"But if she does?" Pitcher queried.

"If she does, an important slice of your case against Frensham will have melted away."

"She'll come back," Lyle repeated. "We can always put a bit of pressure on her if necessary."

"How?" Neve asked, with one eyebrow raised quizzically.

"Through the police out there," Lyle replied.

"If she decides not to return, there's nothing you can do to make her," Neve remarked firmly. He had spent his lifetime working with the police and was well aware of the tendency of some officers to say what they wanted to believe and hope for the best. It was invariably at this particular stage that they were liable to gaze confidently at the horizon and ignore the immediate pitfalls. Sergeant Lyle, Neve now reflected, clearly belonged to that body of officers who was sure everything would turn out all right on the day.

"Supposing for a moment, sir, that she didn't come back and give evidence, would you feel we still had a case against Frensham?"

Neve stared at the doodles he'd been making on his note-pad, while the two officers watched him. Sergeant Lyle's expression seemed to indicate that he was ready to jump into an argument if he didn't get the answer he wanted. Finally, Neve looked up and said in a slowly thoughtful tone:

"Yes, I think you'd still have a case on the strength of the scientific evidence, but it would obviously be a less substantial one. And probably one that could be undermined in various ways."

"Undermined?" Lyle said in what was almost a shocked tone. "In what way undermined, sir?"

"Well, supposing Frensham gives the lie to what the Borg girl told you. Supposing he says that she used to wear his sweater and that she was wearing it the day in question and that it was she who returned home with blood on it."

"Why hasn't he said so before, then?" Lyle asked aggressively.

"Because he didn't want to get her into trouble. He was playing the part of the chivalrous young Englishman."

"You can't really believe that, sir," Lyle said incredulously.

"You're right, but I'm not the jury, am I? Juries, as we know too well, are prone to swallow anything that slips easily down their corporate throat. They won't be particularly anxious to convict a seventeen-year-old youth of murder and if the blame can be slithered off on to this dominant and absent Swedish girl. . . ." He made a helpless gesture. "The point is, it could happen if Kerstin Borg doesn't return."

"I could scarcely prevent her leaving," Pitcher observed glumly.

"Too true," Neve said. "If witnesses don't want to stay around and give evidence, that's it. Should it come to that, it won't be the first time the prosecution has lost a case on that account."

"But what about the evidence of the earrings?" Lyle broke in.

"What does it amount to without Miss Borg's evidence? That she owned such a pair, that the green one was found at the scene and the red one, or something similar to it, was noticed by Sergeant Attwell in Frensham's bedroom. He didn't take possession of it and it has never been seen since. And Sergeant Attwell is an officer under suspicion and therefore, the defence will say, scarcely a witness whose word can be relied on." He glanced from one to the other. "That's right, isn't it?"

Pitcher nodded. "I'm still satisfied that Kersty Borg didn't have anything to do with the murder."

"You might be right, but it won't prevent the defence advancing the sort of line I've been suggesting if she remains out of sight in Sweden during the course of Frensham's trial." He shot Pitcher a quizzical look. "You say that you're satisfied she didn't have any part in the murder, but isn't her admission of washing the sweater evidence of an act done with intent to impede an arrest knowing that an arrestable offence had been committed?"

"There's no evidence, sir, she actually knew that Paul had committed an arrestable offence," Pitcher said stoutly.

Neve smiled. "I take your point. In any event she's obviously more useful as a witness than as a minor defendant. It's probably as well not to probe too deeply into her state of mind as she washed the sweater. But she certainly made a thorough job of it from what the lab said." He put two further lines into his doodle and went on, "Which brings us back to the question that brought you here. Is there enough evidence to charge Paul Frensham with murder? Before I answer that, let me just ask you a question, Mr. Pitcher. Are you convinced that you're on target? That Paul Frensham is your man?"

To Sergeant Lyle's obvious dismay, Pitcher didn't answer immediately. Then he said slowly, "Reasonably certain, sir. Not one hundred percent, but reasonably sure."

"I gather you don't share Mr. Pitcher's reservations?" Neve remarked to Lyle.

"No, sir, I don't. I think Frensham did it and that we ought to be able to convict him."

"Why are you only reasonably certain?" Neve asked, turning back to Pitcher.

"Because we've not yet been able to block all his bolt-holes. But equally I'm in no doubt that he has a case to answer."

"I think so, too," Neve said.

"So we charge him?"

With the faint light of battle in his eyes, Neve merely nodded.

Chapter 16

That same morning, Nick Attwell had just returned from taking Simon out when the phone rang.

"You go, darling," Clare called out from the kitchen. "It's probably for you, anyway."

Making Nick answer the telephone was another part of her devised therapy for him. Anything to frustrate his inclination to withdraw from contact with people.

"Am I speaking to Detective Sergeant Attwell?" a voice enquired in a somewhat solemn tone.

"Yes, speaking."

"This is Detective Chief Superintendent Upperton, sergeant. I expect you can guess why I'm calling you?"

"About the allegation of corruption made against me, sir?"

"Yes, though more specifically to arrange a convenient time for an interview. The sooner the better."

"Any time you care to name, sir."

"Good, good! As a matter of fact I had this afternoon in mind. I take it that would suit you?"

"Yes, I suppose so, sir. I hadn't thought you meant as soon as that."

"Well, let's try this afternoon then," Upperton said, ignoring Nick's comment. "And can you come along here to the Yard? Say, three o'clock?"

There was a pause before Nick said in a pleading tone, "Does it have to be at the Yard, sir? You couldn't come here?"

"You'd prefer not to show your face in this building, is that it?" Upperton asked in a not unkind tone.

"That's about it, sir. If we could meet elsewhere, it would save me a lot of embarrassment."

"May I point out, sergeant, that over a thousand people work in this building? I don't know how many you know by sight, but I suppose I'd recognise an odd fifty or so. It's not as if you're the Commissioner, though I suspect there are quite a few who wouldn't even know him if they met him in a lift. Also, as you know, A.10 occupy a different part of the building from C.1 so the chance of your being recognised is further diminished." He paused. "All in all, while I understand your susceptibilities, I think this would be the best place. I'll expect you at three o'clock."

It was several seconds after Upperton had rung off before Nick replaced his receiver.

"Who was that?" Clare asked, as he came into the kitchen.

"Upperton. I've got to go to the Yard for an interview this afternoon." He looked at her with a stricken expression.

"Well, that's all right, I can look after Simon," Clare replied, deliberately ignoring the strong evidence of self-pity.

"I don't know how I'm going to face stepping into that building."

"The odds are that nobody'll recognise you."

"That's what Upperton said."

"Look, Nick, my darling, just because you've been suspended doesn't mean your face has suddenly become as well known as the prime minister's."

"I still wish I didn't have to go there."

"Did the professor give any indication about the nature of the interview?"

Nick shook his head dolefully. "It'll be to get my answers to specific allegations and generally hear my side of the story."

"I'd expected him to see you sooner," Clare remarked.

"He'll have been looking for outside evidence which might back up Frensham's allegation. The fact that he's ready to see me means he has probably completed his enquiries."

"That's encouraging in itself," Clare said, wiping her hands down the front of her apron as she closed the oven door with her foot.

At half-past two that afternoon Nick found himself sitting in the same café he'd gone to with Alice Macpherson on the day he was suspended. This time he sat there alone, though his mind was in much the same sort of turmoil as it had been on the previous occasion. It was all very well for others to try and jolly him along, but it was he, and not they, who was about to be put on the rack. What, he reflected miserably, had ever induced him to embark upon a career where you could be subjected to slow torture in the cause of propitiating the gods of public opinion?

It was in something of a self-induced state of trance that he entered the Yard building a minute or two before three o'clock. He was hardly through the door when Detective Sergeant Young stepped forward.

"I thought I'd come down and take you up," Young said pleasantly. It was only later Nick realised that this had been nothing less than a thoughtful gesture on Upperton's part.

"Come in and sit down, sergeant," Upperton said, as Nick was shown into his office. He had risen and waved to a chair on the other side of his desk.

He had once been pointed out in the distance to Nick, but this was the first time Nick had seen him at close quarters, and "professor" he certainly was in appearance. Tall, lean figure with a slight stoop, lined bespectacled face and thinning mouse-coloured hair brushed back from a prominent widow's peak. Policeman was the last thing he'd be taken for, in particular a Detective Chief Superintendent.

Nick could see an original statement on the desk in front of Upperton, which he assumed to be that of Paul Frensham.

"I'm sure you'll understand, sergeant, that this interview must be conducted under caution," Upperton said with a small nervous cough. Nick nodded and passed his tongue across his lips which had become suddenly dry. God knows how many times he had administered the caution to others, never dreaming that the day would come when he would be the recipient. He stared at Upperton's face as though mesmerised as the Chief Superintendent went on, "You are not obliged to make any statement or say anything unless you wish to do so, but you must clearly understand that what you do say will be put into writing and may be given in evidence." He paused, turned the pages of the statement in front of him and said, "Now we've got that out of the way, we can begin. I take it, sergeant, that there is no dispute it was you who went to the Frenshams' house on the afternoon in ques-

108

tion and subsequently escorted Paul Frensham to the police station?"

"No dispute at all, sir."

"Did you see anyone else in the house?"

"No, sir."

"That also accords with what young Frensham says. Now perhaps we can get down to detail, starting at the beginning. You rang the bell?"

"Yes, sir."

"And Paul Frensham opened the door?"

"Yes, sir."

"And what did you do then?"

"I told him who I was and that I wanted to speak to him about the death of Mrs. Isaacs."

"And what did he say?"

"He appeared considerably shaken and I suggested it might make it easier if I could come in."

"Yes?"

"And I entered the house."

"Frensham says that you thrust your way in, pushing him up against the wall. What do you say to that?"

"It's quite untrue, sir."

"And what happened after you'd entered?"

"I asked him if he'd been at Mrs. Isaacs' the previous afternoon and he said he had. I then asked him if he'd been inside her house and he denied this, saying he'd only been in the garden. I think it was at this point, sir, that he said he hadn't known Mrs. Isaacs was dead until I told him. I then said that she had been found murdered but I didn't tell him how she'd met her death."

"Yes, what happened next?"

"I said I'd like him to accompany me to the station and he agreed. But he asked if he could go up to his bedroom to fetch his jacket and I said 'yes' but I'd go with him. I suspected he might get up to something, sir, if I let him go alone."

"Did he ask if he might phone his father?"

Nick shifted uncomfortably on his chair. "I think he might have done, sir."

"He says that he asked you and that you refused."

"I think, sir, I procrastinated rather than refused."

"You did know that he was only seventeen?"

"Yes, sir."

"I see. What did you do when you got up to the bedroom?"

"I looked around, sir."

"Searched it?"

"Yes, sir, I suppose it was a search of sorts."

"Frensham says you did so despite his protests that you had no right to."

Nick gave Upperton an appealing look. "I think I did have a right to. If I'd not searched, I wouldn't have found the freshly washed sweater."

But whatever Upperton's private thoughts, he was giving nothing away. He was the deus ex machina asking the questions and recording the answers. Approving or dissenting comments were not for him.

"The sweater was the only article you did take possession of?"

"Yes, sir."

"And then you drove Frensham to the station?"

"Yes, sir."

"Was there any conversation on the way?"

"I don't recall any, sir. Certainly nothing of any significance."

"Frensham says," Upperton went on, "that you suddenly told him you had discovered an important piece of evidence which would clinch the case against him, but that you'd suppress it if he gave you two thousand pounds. What would you like to say about that?"

"That it's a monstrous lie. There's not one word of truth in it." Nick could feel the sweat trickling down his back and forming on his upper lip. He ran an agitated finger across his mouth.

"Can you think of any reason why Frensham should have made this allegation?" Upperton asked in the same quietly neutral tone.

"I can only suggest, sir, that it was a question of attack being the best form of defence."

"I understand that you have recently recalled seeing a red object in Frensham's bedroom which might have been the counterpart of the green earring found at the scene of the murder."

"That's correct, sir."

"If it was the counterpart earring, it was a vital piece of evidence?"

"Yes, sir. That's why I called Chief Inspector Pitcher as soon as its significance dawned on me."

"But you didn't take possession of it?"

Nick's face dropped as the implication of Upperton's question flooded his mind.

"No, sir, because, as I've said, I only realised its significance later."

"Meanwhile, of course, it has vanished. A possibly vital piece of evidence against Frensham has vanished."

"But I've explained, sir," Nick said in a tone of urgent pleading.

Upperton gave a non-committal nod.

"Is there anything further you want to say?"

"No, sir, except that it's the most diabolical allegation ever to be made against an officer."

The phone on Upperton's desk rang and he stretched out a hand for the receiver.

"Detective Chief Superintendent Upperton speaking . . . good afternoon to you . . . I see . . . well, thank you for letting me know . . . yes, it will affect my investigation . . . good-bye."

For a time he held the telephone receiver poised over its rest while he stared into the middle distance. Then dropping it into place, he looked at Nick and said, "That was Detective Chief Inspector Pitcher. Paul Frensham has just been arrested and charged with the murder of Mrs. Isaacs." He paused before adding, "I'm afraid that'll mean, sergeant, my enquiries into his allegation will now go into cold storage until his trial is over."

Chapter 17

When Detective Chief Inspector Pitcher arrived at the Magistrates' Court the next morning in order to apply for a formal remand of the case, he found the entrance besieged by reporters and a television news crew.

As the case itself hardly merited such public interest, it seemed obvious that Sir Guy must be responsible.

Paul Frensham had spent the night in a cell at the police station and been driven to court about half an hour before Pitcher arrived. He was now, Pitcher was informed by the gaoler, closeted with his father, a solicitor and counsel.

"What on earth do they want counsel for on a formal remand?" Pitcher exclaimed.

"Name of Croxley," the gaoler said.

"Never heard of him."

"Wait till you see him!" the gaoler remarked darkly.

"What's special about him?"

"Looks like he's come to address the House of Lords. Black jacket and striped trousers and stiff white collar. Even has a gold watch chain strung across his paunch. Walked in here and began making demands as if he was used to people falling in front of his feet for the honour of being trodden on."

"Well, I reckon he'll have had a wasted journey today," Pitcher said with a shrug. "Who's sitting as chairman this morning?"

"Mrs. Dowell. You won't have any trouble from her."

At ten o'clock, the magistrates took their seats, Mrs. Dowell flanked by two men, one surprisingly youthful, the other near to retirement age. All three, while contriving to look at ease, wore expressions of expectancy.

The public area of the court was filled to capacity and the press bench was crammed to overflowing.

Mr. Newsome, the clerk of the Court, surveyed the scene with the slightly sardonic air of a lecturer who knows quite well that his capacity audience has been drawn by an ulterior motive. He allowed his glance to rest for a moment on Mr. Croxley who was laying out a battery of coloured pens on the desk in front of him. Then his eye went to the piece of paper which the court usher had given him and which informed him that defending counsel was Mr. Warren Croxley instructed by Messrs. Hillary, Woodside and Hastings. He stood up and turned to have a short whispered conversation with the three magistrates before facing about and announcing that the court would first deal with the case of Paul Frensham.

At the same moment as Pitcher stepped into the witness box, Clare squeezed herself into the back of the court, out of breath having run the last hundred yards to arrive in time, and Mr. Croxley rose ponderously to his feet.

"Your worships," he said in a thick syrupy tone which was his normal Court voice, "I represent the accused in this matter."

Mrs. Dowell gave him a small nod of acknowledgment, but Mr. Newsome, who was apt to show a faint resentment at new faces in his court, turned immediately to Pitcher and said, "You have an application to make, Mr. Pitcher?"

"Yes, sir. I apply for a week's remand in custody. The accused was only charged yesterday afternoon and the case is not yet ready to go ahead. In due course the papers will be referred to the Director of Public Prosecutions who will undertake the conduct of the prosecution."

"Is there any objection to a week's remand in custody?" Mr. Newsome enquired, looking reluctantly in Mr. Croxley's direction.

"The strongest possible objection, your worships," defending counsel declared, staring determinedly over the top of the clerk's head. "Not to the remand itself," he went on, "but to it being in custody. I would like to ask the officer a few questions before I make an application for bail for this young accused."

"It's very unusual for bail to be granted in murder cases," Mr. Newsome observed in an offhand tone.

"Unusual perhaps, but by no means without precedent."

"Ask Mr. Pitcher your questions then," Mrs. Dowell broke in tactfully.

"Is it a fact, officer, that my client is a mere seventeen years old?" Mr. Croxley said, fixing Pitcher with a stern look.

"Yes, sir."

"Do you accept that his father is a well-known public figure?"

"Yes, sir."

"Do you have any fears that my client might repeat his crime if allowed on bail?"

"Commit another murder, do you mean?" Pitcher asked in surprise.

"That is precisely what I mean."

"No, I haven't any reason to think he would."

"I'm obliged to you, officer," Mr. Croxley said with a gracious inclination of his head. "Do you have any reason to suppose he might abscond if granted bail?"

"Yes, I believe he might," Pitcher said quietly after a pause in which he became aware that everyone was looking at him.

"Oh, come now, officer," Mr. Croxley said in an outraged tone. "Are you seriously suggesting that he might disappear in order to avoid the hearing of this case?"

"Yes, sir."

"This boy of seventeen, the son of a famous father! I invite you to reconsider your answer."

"I don't need to."

"Very well," Mr. Croxley said grimly. "Let me just ask you one further question: should their worships grant bail to my client, may I take it that you would not have anxieties about interference with witnesses?"

There was another pause before Pitcher answered. He believed that any interference with witnesses was likely to come from father rather than from son. Just as he thought that if Paul Frensham absconded, it would be at his father's instigation.

Resting his gaze on Mrs. Dowell, he said, "I think, your worship, that there is a possibility of witnesses being interfered with in this case."

Mrs. Dowell gave him a fleeting smile as if to indicate that she understood what lay behind his answer.

"Have you any further questions to ask the witness?" Mr. Newsome asked in a bored tone.

Mr. Croxley, who had been engaged in feverish whisperings with Mr. Woodside and Sir Guy sitting behind him, now turned and faced the magistrates and their clerk once more.

"I have no further questions, but now propose to address their worships," he said, glaring at Mr. Newsome, who ostentatiously consulted his watch.

"Yes, Mr. Croxley," Mrs. Dowell broke in, well used to the role of pacifist in the court over which she presided with competence and quiet courtesy.

Adopting a somewhat oratorical stance, Mr. Croxley began his plea.

"I accept, your worships, that it is unusual for bail to be granted where the charge is murder, but, as I pointed out to your clerk when he interrupted me earlier, it is by no means without precedent, provided there are special reasons to justify such a course. And this case abounds in special reasons. First, the defendant is a mere seventeen years old, still a boy in the eyes of those of us who are ourselves parents. Secondly, he comes from a first class home in which, of course, he will continue to reside under parental control if you accede to my application. You will have noted that I asked the officer three questions: *the* three questions which are relevant to a consideration of bail. Is there likely to be any repetition of the offence to which there could only be one truthful answer: no. Is he likely to abscond to which the officer gave the quite unsupported and unconvincing reply that he might. I *ask* you, madam, do you really believe that the son of this eminent father is likely to abscond? I suggest it is beyond all probability that he would do so and I invite you to ignore any insinuation to the contrary. And the third question was whether the officer feared my client might interfere with witnesses if released and to that you may think you were given a somewhat equivocal and unsatisfactory reply. This is not a case involving gang-type criminals and underworld figures: it's a case of a boy facing a charge of murder which he utterly denies and which he will contest every inch of the way. This is not the sort of case in which you get interference with witnesses, and I ask you to put any such suggestion out of your heads as both unproven and unworthy." Mr. Croxley gave his paunch a small, thoughtful pat and pushed his spectacles further back up his nose. "You have before you, your worships, a young lad of excellent background who suddenly finds himself enmeshed with the law. Are you really going to order that he must be carted off to a common jail, there to undergo the appalling traumas that inevitably await a sensitive young man locked up in a grey Victorian fortress? Are you really going to order that?"

It was perhaps an unfortunate question as Mr. Newsome immediately seized on it and said in a bored tone, "There are plenty of seventeen-year-olds awaiting trial in custody. Moreover, special provision is made for them."

"It would be discourteous of me, your worships, to enter into argument with your clerk when I'm in the process of addressing you," Mr. Croxley said, keeping his gaze well above the level of Mr. Newsome's head. "I ask you to give this application the most solemn and serious consideration. And should, as I hope, you see fit to grant my client bail, I need hardly add that he will be prepared to abide by any conditions that you wish to impose. I have already said that he will continue to live at home under parental control. He will report daily to the police if you wish to make that a condition." At this point, Mr. Woodside half rose in his seat behind defending counsel and hissed something in his ear. "I am much obliged," Mr. Croxley said to the court at large. "I am instructed that my client possesses a passport in his own name and he will, of course, be ready to surrender that to the police as a further safeguard against his disappearance, if anyone takes that as a serious possibility, which I assure you again it is not."

Defending counsel sat down and turned to whisper to Sir Guy whose flinching expression seemed to indicate that Mr. Croxley might suffer from bad breath.

Mrs. Dowell spoke briefly to her two colleagues and then announced, "The Court will retire to consider the application."

Everyone rose as the three magistrates trouped out to their private room.

Clare took advantage of the general movement to achieve a better position. She had so far been able to see only the back of Paul Frensham's head and she was determined to see the face of this young man who had set out to destroy her husband.

By dint of a certain amount of pushing and squeezing she reached a position level with the dock from which she was at least able to see him in profile. He was leaning forward while his solicitor and father

116

were talking to him over the top of the dock. He was frowning and kept on sniffing as though he had a head cold.

Clare found herself thinking that he was almost exactly as she expected him to look from Nick's description. Good-looking in a baby-faced way but with an expression which said "spoilt" as clearly as if it had been spelt out in neon.

For several seconds Clare stared at him with hatred for what he'd done to Nick. She didn't like him any better for having killed an old lady, but at least that had been relatively swift compared with the slow torture he had inflicted on her husband.

Since Nick's return home from Scotland Yard the previous evening, he had been in a terrible state, worse than immediately after his suspension. It was Upperton's questions about the red earring, and their insinuation, which had thrown him back into a well of despair and hopelessness.

It had taxed all Clare's own resources not to join him there. But in the course of a sleepless night for both of them, she had decided she must go on as she had begun; if now almost as much for the sake of her own morale as his. She was still haunted, however, by Nick's expression of wordless reproach when she told him at breakfast that she would be out for most of the morning.

Whether Paul Frensham was or was not given bail was as inconsequential as the colour of his socks compared with what he had wrought in her life.

She wrenched her gaze from Frensham and allowed it to roam round the court-room. There was no one she recognised, not that she'd expected otherwise. She had liked the look of Pitcher, who had an air of quiet competence. Indeed, there had to be more to him than to have reached the rank of detective chief inspector at such an early age. He was now standing against the wall on the far side of the court exchanging an occasional word with someone who, Clare decided, was probably Detective Sergeant Lyle.

Her gaze moved on, eventually returning to Paul Frensham who was nervously biting a thumb nail while his father and solicitor were talking to each other just in front of him. He gave the impression of having switched off from their conversation.

There was certainly no sign of Unsworth, not that Clare had expected to see him. Indeed, his presence would have caused her considerable surprise.

The thought of him now brought a frown to her face. Somehow

she felt that she had let an opportunity slip through her fingers when she had thrust her company on him the evening before last. An initiative had been lost and yet she didn't see what more she could have done to force information from him.

At the beginning when she felt, and he seemed to recognise, that she had the upper hand, he had admitted he had gone back to the house to look for something.

"Something in Mrs. Isaacs' bedroom?" Clare had pressed him.

"Work it out for yourself, lady," he had replied.

Clare had, and had decided that it must be something in the bedroom as that was where she had discovered him.

"What was it?"

"Let's just say it was a piece of paper."

"I want to know what?"

"Sorry."

"Was it a will?"

He had given her a foxy grin.

"Not a bad guess."

"So it *was* a will?"

"I didn't say so."

"But was it?"

"You're neither hot nor cold and that's all I'm saying."

"Why were you searching for it?"

"That'd be telling."

"If you don't tell me, I'll go to the police."

He had shaken his head. "I don't think you will."

"I most certainly will."

"Look, lady, as soon as you leave this place, you've lost me forever. You can't remove me physically to the police station and all I have to do after you've gone is move to a different address. And I shall make sure that I don't drop any more bits of paper when you're around. You don't hold as many trump cards as you pretend."

It had been at this stage that Clare had become aware of her loss of initiative.

"I could still go to the police and tell them enough to make them step up their search for you," she had replied. "Enough to make them regard you as a serious suspect."

"I could prove an alibi."

"The sort of alibi you could produce would soon be broken. Anyway how is it you know the exact time for which you'd require an alibi? That in itself is suspicious."

"I don't have to go on sitting here listening to you, lady," he had said with a note of anger.

"Was your row with Mrs. Isaacs connected with the piece of paper you were looking for the other evening?"

"Who said I had a row with Mrs. Isaacs?"

"It's common knowledge. That's why the police want to see you."

"I don't want anything to do with the police."

"Then you must help me."

"I've told you all I can."

"It's not enough."

"Will you leave me alone if I tell you more?" he had asked after a pause during which he had sat frowning furiously at the remnants of his meal.

"That depends."

"My row with Mrs. I. had nothing to do with her death."

"So you say!"

"And that's all I'm saying!"

He had pushed back his chair and stood up.

"Who did murder her?" Clare had asked urgently. "I have to know. My employers need to know. It could affect the administration of her will."

He had given her a curious look. "Why are you asking me that? Why not the police?"

"The police are still investigating," she had said lamely.

"Are you on a newspaper?"

"No, I told you, I'm . . . ."

"I know what you told me and I don't believe you. You're just snooping. I don't know why but I don't like it."

And for the second time in the space of a few days he had walked out on her. As soon as he reached the pavement he had begun to run. By the time Clare was out of the café he had disappeared.

She had gone immediately to the address in Malabar Road, but there'd been no sign of him. Like a bird frightened away from its nest, he was obviously not going to return there so long as he believed Clare was still around.

It had been in a mood of frustration that she had returned home.

She had been going over and over their conversation in her mind ever since it had taken place, always in the hope of squeezing some further meaning from his words.

What could the piece of paper be that had drawn him back to the dead woman's house on a furtive mission? Not a will, he had said.

Whatever it was obviously affected someone still alive. Affected that person in an important way, too; otherwise why all the trouble? Of course, it was possible that it was something affecting Unsworth himself: something which, if found by the police, could reflect against him. It seemed a reasonable, if not irrefutable, inference that the mysterious piece of paper was connected with the row which had led to Unsworth being thrown out of the house.

Clare wondered whether the police were still looking for him as keenly as before Frensham's arrest. Probably not. They presumably regarded his disappearance as one of those untidy loose ends that most crimes provide. But it had not been enough to deter them from charging Paul Frensham with the murder.

She glanced once more across to where Pitcher and Lyle were standing. It was very tempting to go over and introduce herself and see what she could learn. But common sense told her that their reaction would be first surprise and then suspicion about what had brought this suspended colleague's wife to court from the other side of London. At best they would be polite but uncommunicative.

Her thoughts went back to Unsworth. He had not only returned to the dead woman's house looking for something, but he had let himself in with a key. That meant he had retained a key and the only reason for doing that was because he'd always intended coming back.

And what of the third person in the house that night? Had he been looking for the same thing? She tried to compare Paul Frensham with the figure which had dashed past her in the driveway. The trouble was that she had received scarcely any useful impression at all. It had just been a male figure moving very rapidly. Perhaps a young rather than an old person, but that was about all she had had time to register.

She glanced at her watch. The magistrates had been deliberating for over ten minutes. It was unusual enough for bail applications to be made in murder cases and even more extraordinary for a court to take so long to reach what must surely be a foregone conclusion. She decided they were probably protracting their absence for appearance's sake. So as not to give Sir Guy Frensham any ammunition for one of his future programmes.

The power of the media could be inhibiting, oppressive as well as salutary.

A door opened and an usher called for silence as the three magistrates resumed their seats on the bench.

Mr. Newsome came in through a different door and held a brief whispered conversation with Mrs. Dowell before sitting down himself.

"We have given this application the most careful consideration," the chairman announced, "and have decided that there are exceptional circumstances which would justify us in granting bail to the accused." She turned to look at Pitcher who was standing just behind the witness box. "Will you help us about sureties and conditions, Mr. Pitcher? We are minded to order that he shall report daily to the police and surrender his passport. As he is only seventeen, his own recognisance is probably no more than a formality, but what about other sureties?"

Pitcher, who was not entirely taken by surprise, said that the police would be willing to accept Sir Guy's recognisance alone provided it was in a substantial sum.

"Then we'll allow bail on the conditions we've mentioned, with, in addition, the accused entering into his own recognisance in the sum of ten pounds and a surety in the sum of ten thousand pounds." She peered at Mr. Croxley who had been in a flurried consultation with Mr. Woodside and Sir Guy.

"Sir Guy Frensham will stand surety in the sum mentioned, your worships, and he has asked me to give you his personal guarantee that his son will answer to his bail whenever required."

Mrs. Dowell turned back to Pitcher. "How long a remand do you need, Mr. Pitcher, before you'll be ready to proceed?"

"I would hope we could get our file to the D.P.P. within a month. It then rests with him."

Mr. Croxley was back on his feet, not bothering to conceal his expression of triumph. He had no doubt that it was the power of his advocacy which had persuaded the court to accede to his plea. This was particularly galling to Mr. Newsome who knew otherwise but couldn't say so. The influencing factors had, in fact, been Frensham's age, a feeling that if anyone ought to be remanded in custody for the reasons given by the police it was his father rather than him, and a recent powerful reminder from the Home Secretary that magistrates should not be too negative in their approach to bail; that the prisons were over-cluttered with people in custody awaiting trial.

"I think it must be apparent to your worships," defending counsel said in a tone as dark as treacle coffee, "that this case will be fought every inch of the way. The defence will yield nothing and are determined to clear this young man's name at the earliest possible moment. We shall therefore be opting for full committal proceedings with each and every witness giving oral evidence in this court and being subjected to rigorous cross-examination. That means . . . ."

"What you're saying," Mr. Newsome broke in impatiently, "is that you won't accept a paper committal on service of witnesses' statements. I'm sure Detective Chief Inspector Pitcher will convey that to the D.P.P. It means, of course, that instead of the case occupying a matter of minutes in this court, it'll take up days, with all the consequent dislocation of work."

Mr. Croxley had listened to this acerbic approach with pursed lips.

"I am sorry, your worships," he went on, "that your clerk appears to equate the interests of justice with getting through the court list as quickly as possible. However much I might regret any dislocation of the work in this court, I could not allow such a consideration to weigh with me where my client's interests are concerned. I am sure *you* will understand that," he added, fixing Mrs. Dowell with a grave look.

"We all understand," she said tactfully. "I am sure the necessary arrangements for the hearing will be made to everyone's satisfaction. Mr. Newsome is very skilled at juggling the court's work load," she added, smiling sweetly at the top of the clerk's head.

A few minutes later, Paul Frensham was stepping from the dock, a broad smirk on his face. It was fortunate, Clare reflected, that she didn't have an egg or a ripe tomato to hand or she would certainly have thrown it at him.

"They out of their minds?" Sergeant Lyle muttered to Pitcher as they pushed their way out of court. "What the hell do they think they're doing granting bail on a murder charge?"

Pitcher, however, merely shrugged. "I don't think it matters very much."

"Not matter! It's the principle of the thing. Bail for murder, indeed." He shook his head in the manner of one for whom there are no surprises left.

"I doubt whether Paul Frensham will get up to much," Pitcher remarked. "It's his father who'll create all the mischief. He's already begun and I don't imagine he's finished."

"Well, you know my views about him. I'd just love to feel his collar."

It was some time later when they were driving back to the station after completion of the various bail formalities that Sergeant Lyle said, "You're not really worried that we've got the wrong man, are you, guv'nor?"

Pitcher didn't reply at once. Then, with a small, fatalistic shrug, he said, "I hope we haven't—for Nick Attwell's sake."

Chapter 18

Pitcher hadn't long been back at the station that morning when he received a phone call from a Mr. Wystan, manager of the branch of the City and Provincial Bank which had carried Mrs. Isaacs' account.

"I thought I ought to let you know at once," the bank manager said in a tone which bordered on the officious, "that Mrs. Isaacs' house appears to have been broken into. When one of my staff went there this morning to start making an inventory, he found her bedroom in a state of disorder. Later he discovered that a kitchen window had been forced. As you will be aware," he went on, "the bank was appointed executor of her will."

"Was your man able to say whether anything had been taken?"

"No, he was not. Mrs. Isaacs was a considerable hoarder and I doubt whether anyone could tell. What chiefly concerns me is the fact that the house could be broken into. Surely you've had a man keeping an eye on it?"

"No, we've not," Pitcher replied, stifling the more abrasive comment that Mr. Wystan's tone brought to the tip of his tongue. "Once we'd completed our examination of the premises, that was that. I'm afraid we don't have manpower available to guard premises merely because a murder has taken place there."

"Well, it seems most unfortunate."

"I agree and I'll have somebody go round immediately. There may be some fingerprints. Meanwhile, as executor, your bank had better make additional arrangements to protect the property, Mr. Wystan. It's your responsibility."

"I'll have to take the matter up with my head office," the bank manager said in a deflated tone. "Incidentally, I see you've arrested the young man who used to do some gardening for the deceased."

"Yes, Paul Frensham."

"Is it permissible to ask whether you have a strong case against him?"

"Reasonably strong."

"I think the bank will probably wish to be represented at court."

"For what purpose?"

"Just to watch the proceedings. It'll be up to head office, but I shall recommend that we have counsel with a watching brief."

It didn't matter to Pitcher one way or the other, but he was glad he wasn't a beneficiary under the will, obliged to watch the assets frittered away on legal fees.

It was mid-afternoon before Sergeant Lyle whom, with Detective Constable Bax, he had despatched to Teeling Road, reported back.

"Kitchen window had been forced all right," Lyle announced, flopping into Pitcher's spare chair. "The woodwork was splintered, but I've had a cast taken of the indentation marks, for what it's worth. The old girl's bedroom seemed to be the only room that had been disturbed, but, as her bank manager said, it was impossible to tell whether anything had been taken."

"Fingerprints?"

"One or two good ones on the chest of drawers. Otherwise nothing but a lot of smudged prints. Particularly in the area of the forced window. I had the impression that someone had done a wiping job."

"But not in the bedroom itself?"

"Not round the chest of drawers, anyway."

"Well, all we can do is see whether the computer comes up with anything. If it doesn't, I can't see us getting any farther. It could have been just a casual burglar who knew the house was empty."

Lyle nodded. "That's what it looked like to me, guv'nor."

The next day, however, a telex message reached the station indicating that the fingerprints appeared to be those of an Anthony Rivings, 26 Filby Street, N.10. It also gave his C.R.O. file number. Indeed, if the prints had not been those of someone with a criminal record, the computer's search would have been negative. There were of course rare occasions when a whole town or district was fingerprinted, but always with the firm assurance that the prints of those eliminated from the enquiry in question would be destroyed.

"We'll get a search warrant," Pitcher said, "and go along this evening when he's back from work."

"I'm wondering if it wasn't Rivings who put Frensham up to a bit of theft, in the course of which the old girl got killed?" Lyle said thoughtfully.

"Could be," Pitcher remarked. "It's worth exploring."

It was already dark when they pulled up outside 26 Filby Street at 6 o'clock that misty October evening.

On this occasion, the door was opened by Tony Rivings himself.

"We want to ask you some more questions, Tony," Pitcher said. "We've also got a search warrant."

"What the bleeding . . . . ?"

"You left your prints at Mrs. Isaacs' house. What'd you take, Tony?"

"I didn't take nothing."

"We'll still have a look around."

"Can't we talk somewhere else?" he asked anxiously.

"Sure, back at the station. After we've had a look around. Anyone else at home?"

"My kid sister. In the kitchen."

"Tell her a couple of your friends have called; then show us your bedroom."

With Rivings rooted like a poleaxed young ox in the doorway, the two officers searched his bedroom, but without finding anything of apparent significance. Later they searched the other rooms of the house with diminishing thoroughness and finally the kitchen after Rivings had sent his sister out to get him a packet of cigarettes.

"O.K., now we'll get back to the station," Pitcher said, their search completed.

"How long'll I be there?"

"Can't tell you, Tony. Could be a time. We've quite a bit to talk about." Observing Rivings' expression, Pitcher added, "I'll see your mother gets a message if necessary."

"She'll do her nut when she hears."

"I'd have thought she was used to it in her family, Tony," Sergeant Lyle said amiably.

Rivings scowled. "Spare me the funnies, will you!"

For the first part of the journey no one in the car spoke. Then Rivings, who had been staring out of the window with a heavy frown, said, "I didn't take a bloody thing from the house."

"Tell us more, but first I'd better caution you," Lyle said quickly.

"Bugger the caution."

"I'd like to, but you know what judges are."

"Bloody hell, you haven't charged me and you're already talking about bloody judges." He shot Pitcher a sidelong glance. "I'll do a deal with you, mister. I'll tell you all I know if you drop any charges against me."

"All you know about what, Tony?"

"About what you want to know about."

"Mrs. Isaacs' death, you mean?"

"Could be."

"What do you know about it?"

A look of cunning flitted across Rivings' face. "I might be able to help you quite a lot."

"Give evidence against Paul Frensham, is that what you have in mind?"

"Depends, doesn't it?"

Rivings' background and record did nothing to inspire Pitcher with any confidence in his reliability as a witness and he had no intention of doing any sort of deal with him and certainly not one which involved handing him a blank cheque.

"What were you looking for when you broke into Mrs. Isaacs' house, Tony?"

"I just went in to have a scout around."

"And opened all the drawers in her bedroom?"

"Thought there might be a bit of cash lying around that no one would miss."

"And was there?"

"I've already told you, I didn't nick a thing."

"Because you didn't find anything?"

"Didn't have much bleeding time, did I?"

"What's that supposed to mean?"

"Another bleeding geezer comes on the scene."

"Let me get this straight," Pitcher said slowly. "Are you telling us that while you were in the house, someone else broke in?"

"Must have done."

"Who?"

"Can't even tell you if he had two heads or one. The house wasn't exactly floodlit, you know. It was as black as a beetle's belly in there."

"What did you do?"

"Got out."

"Did you speak to the other person?"

A sly grin was switched on and off Rivings' face.

"No, I didn't stop to speak to him."

"Did he know of *your* presence in the house?"

"Can't say."

"Are you willing to make a statement about this?"

"If you like."

"It's up to you."

"If I do, how'll you help me?"

"Say you didn't give us any trouble."

"Is that bleeding all?"

"What else do you expect?"

"Bail. If you can get bail for murder these days, you must be able to get it for just taking a look round a house."

"Just taking a look round a house is called burglary with intent in your case."

"You're not going to keep me inside, are you?"

Pitcher shrugged. "Serious charge, bad record."

"But what about bloody Paul Frensham getting bail?"

"That wasn't our fault."

"Just because his bloody father's a sir, I suppose."

"What's Paul told you about the murder?"

"You asked me that last time."

"I know and you said you wanted time to think. You've now had time."

"All I know is that Paul was at the house that afternoon."

"We all know that."

"He clammed up about what happened."

"I don't believe you, Tony."

"It's the truth, mister."

"How soon afterwards did you see him?"

"Not for two or three days."

"And he didn't tell you then what had happened?"

"No. He just said there were pickings to be had in the house now that it was empty."

"Was that what took you there?"

"You could say so."

"Did he say what sort of pickings?"

"Cash. He said the old girl left money around in drawers and inside books and under things."

"Had Paul nicked cash in the past?"

"You'd better ask him that."

"I'm asking you."

"He could have had a bit."

"Do you think the Swedish girl knows what happened?"

"She'd know more than me," Rivings said eagerly. "Paul practically wore himself out in her bed." He paused. "Look, mister, I'll probably never see Paul again. We was friends of a sort for a time, but it's all over now. I don't wish him any harm, as long as he don't try and shove me in the mess. I don't think he will, though I'd not put it past bloody Sir Guy."

It was a sentiment which Pitcher shared, though he refrained from voicing his agreement.

The car turned into the station yard and they clambered out. Tony Rivings glanced about him with an expression of bovine resignation before Lyle steered him toward the back entrance of the station.

Pitcher led the way up to the C.I.D. section on the first floor. He felt reasonably satisfied that Rivings had told the broad truth of his escapade. He was less certain that he had told them everything he knew about the murder, though, on the whole, was inclined to believe that he had.

"You'll have to stop the night in a cell," Pitcher said, when the formalities had been completed, "but we won't oppose bail when you come up in court in the morning."

"You can occupy the same cell your friend slept in last night," Lyle said cheerfully.

Rivings grimaced. "What about letting my mum know?"

"What do you want her told?" Pitcher asked.

"I don't want her rushing round here."

"That suits us, too. So what are we going to tell her?"

"I could say that I'm at my girl-friend's."

"O.K. Do you want to use a phone?" Rivings' expression was one of surprise. "What, phone from here?"

"If you want."

"Thanks."

Sergeant Lyle gave Pitcher a surreptitious wink and received one back.

If Tony Rivings did have anything else to divulge, kindness was most likely to ease it out. It was a quality which always came as a surprise to anyone just arrested and charged and could, therefore, work as a most effective persuader on occasions.

Chapter 19

But, in fact, nothing more was learnt from Tony Rivings and the next morning he appeared briefly in the Magistrates' Court to be remanded on bail to a date ahead.

Pitcher would have been willing for the charge to be dealt with by the magistrates, but, as force had been used in his gaining entry to Teeling Road, the case would in due course have to go forward for trial at the Crown Court. In Pitcher's view this was a waste of time and money.

The older Sergeant Lyle was far from agreeing, however, and took the view that Rivings deserved to be put out of circulation for a year or two. He held his Detective Chief Inspector in considerable regard and was not one of those who resented his rapid promotion. Nevertheless, he was not won over to the more enlightened views on punishment of his senior officer. In Lyle's opinion, hanging and birching should both be brought back, to deter as well as to satisfy society's demand for retribution which never lay far below the surface.

Pitcher who found most arguments on the subject stereotyped and unproductive did his best to avoid being drawn into them.

130

In the weeks which followed, his time and that of his team was spent in assembling a file for submission to the D.P.P. A considerable number of witness statements had to be obtained, a task which always took longer than expected, and Pitcher himself had to write his covering report.

However, eventually it was ready for delivery and Pitcher and Lyle took it themselves and handed it over to Mr. Neve, who on this occasion introduced them to the member of his staff assigned to handle the case in the Magistrates' Court.

This was a Mr. Jude, who wore a friendly but competent air. He rubbed his hands with pleasure when told that the defence were insisting on all the witnesses giving their evidence in person at the Magistrates' Court.

"Splendid," he said with a cheerful grin. "Sometimes I think I've become nothing more than a postman. I just carry a great wad of papers to court, hand them in and the defendant's committed for trial quicker than you can say Old Bailey."

"Don't rejoice too soon, Jim," Mr. Neve remarked. "You'll have that old flanneler Croxley against you."

But this piece of news seemed only to enhance Jude's enjoyment of the prospect.

"He's all right," he said indulgently, "though I confess I'd have expected Sir Guy Frensham to have procured the services of one of our trendier brethren in the law."

"Croxley's no fool," Neve observed, "he's just a pain in the rump."

"He got Frensham bail, which was a scandal," Lyle remarked sourly.

"He's not broken any of the conditions of his bail so far, has he?" Neve enquired. Pitcher shook his head. "Well, no harm has ensued."

"It's still a scandal, sir. And it's wrong in my view that the police can't appeal against a decision of that sort."

"But you can in the sense that if he breaks a condition, you can haul him back into court and ask for his bail to be withdrawn."

"But supposing he doesn't give you the excuse to do that?"

"It would seem to show that the magistrates' decision was right in the first place," Neve said with a smile. "But tell me now about Kerstin Borg. Is she going to return?"

"I'm keeping my fingers crossed, sir," Pitcher replied.

"But you're not too hopeful, I gather?"

"We've kept in touch with her and she still says she'll come back, but when it actually gets to it . . . . well, I just wonder."

"You don't have any evidence that she's been got at by the Frenshams?"

"No, I asked her to let me know at once if they tried to dissuade her from coming back to give evidence and she said she would . . . ." He gave a resigned shrug. "But again I wouldn't be too certain."

"Then we can only hope. Her evidence about the sweater and her earrings is extremely important. It provides the sort of cement the prosecution's case needs. In fact," he went on thoughtfully, "one might say that with her evidence the prosecution's case resembles the little pig's house which was built of bricks. Without her evidence, however, it is more akin to the one built of sticks. And we all know what happened to that."

And on this foreboding note, the conference ended.

During this same period, Clare watched Nick's spirits see-saw from day to day.

The trouble was that her own initiative had dried up and she had been unable to take her own enquiries any further. Derek Unsworth had once more gone to ground and it seemed unlikely that chance would ever blow him across her path again.

She had another meeting with Alice Macpherson which had been agreeable but which had achieved nothing. Indeed, Clare had only arranged it because she thought it would help to relieve her sense of frustration at having no other line to pursue.

Alice Macpherson's news, secondhand at that, had been to the effect that Paul Frensham was maintaining a low profile: that he scarcely went out, other than in the company of his father: and that he was certainly not being seen in Joe's Disco or other similar haunts.

In the circumstances, Clare decided not to tell Nick what she had been up to. He would almost certainly be critical, if nothing worse, and, as her endeavours to help him had fizzled out like a wet firecracker, there was no point in adding to his mental burden.

The only member of the household who remained cheerful throughout this period was Simon. Happily, he was too young to be affected by Nick's moods, other than to respond with a swift one of his own when he wanted his father's attention.

Just occasionally Nick would snap at him, but Simon was good enough to regard it as an aberration which could be overlooked. He even accepted the odd light smack with no more than the statutory allowance of tears and this was so whether the punishment was justified or not.

It was about a week before the hearing in the magistrates' court came on that Nick received a phone call from Sergeant Lyle informing him that the D.P.P. required him to give evidence.

He had, of course, always realised that this was more than a possibility, but when the prospect actually materialised into a certainty, he was filled with apprehension.

His evidence was short, but it was still a vital link in the prosecution's case and was, therefore, bound to be attacked in cross-examination. And how else than by seeking to discredit the witness who gave it?

"It's going to be worse than standing in the pillory," he said to Clare, who sought for words of reassurance but found none.

"I know, darling," she said. "It'll be an ordeal, but you'll come through it. Just think of all the people rooting for you." She hesitated, then said, "I want to come to court myself."

"What on earth for?" he asked in amazement. "Anyway, how can you? You'll be looking after Simon."

"I can make arrangements for Simon. I think one of us should be in court all the time just to hear what's said and as you're a witness, you can't be there until you're actually called. So it has to be me."

"But what is there to hear?"

"The whole case against this young man who's made a false allegation against you. Isn't that enough? I'll be there holding a watching brief for you."

Nick shook his head doubtfully. "I don't like it. What're people going to think?"

"What people? And, anyway, nobody's going to recognise me. Moreover, what's it matter if they do?"

Nick turned away and Clare could see that further persuasion on her part was going to be required. Though now that she had made the proposal to Nick, she had no intention of yielding.

And so the date of the court hearing against Paul Frensham approached without further untoward incident.

That is, until the day before.

Chapter 20

"Let's go to that place," Terry said to his friend Philip who was eleven and two years older than himself.

The two boys lived with their respective families in a block of flats near Wandsworth Bridge and were inseparable friends. Though Terry was the brighter boy, he accepted the leadership of his stronger friend.

Together they had explored every inch of the neighbourhood, burrowing through fences and climbing over forbidden walls in the course of countless adventures.

But their favourite haunt was undoubtedly "that place", as it was always referred to.

Just west of the bridge on the south side of the river was a desolate acreage of wasteland which was awaiting re-development. Its northern edge lay along the river where there was a grimy quayside and a rusty iron ladder which led down to mud flats at low tide.

It was the mud flats which were known to Philip and Terry as "that place". At high tide they were covered by eight or ten feet of water, but each time the tide receded and left them exposed, a new and fascinating deposit of flotsam was left high, if not exactly dry.

Like a couple of modern mudlarks, the two boys would pass happy hours picking over the sodden remnants of people's lives. There was seldom anything actually worth taking, but hope of ultimate treasure remained unquenchable.

Just to underline his leadership, Philip appeared to consider the suggestion for a second or two before nodding.

The only tricky part was getting inside the area, which had to be accomplished without being spotted by anyone in authority. But this done, they ran, walked and skipped across the uneven ground in the direction of the river, after pausing to examine some discarded item on their way.

A favourite game was to find something like an old kettle and use it as a target for stone throwing.

On this particular morning, it was low tide and the mud flats stretched twenty feet below them, dark and glistening.

For a time they lay peering over the edge of the one-time quay. Once when they had been standing there, river police had shouted at them to move away, so now they made their initial reconnaissance in a lying position.

Terry suddenly clutched at Philip's arm.

"Looks like a body along there on the right," he said, excitedly.

"Come on," Philip replied, springing to his feet and making for the rusty ladder that was fastened to the wall of the quay.

Terry followed him down and let out a small voluptuous exclamation as he dropped from the final rung into the squelching mud which came half way up his wellingtons.

The object resembling a body lay about twenty yards along to their right and was near the water's edge where the mud was at its wettest and most treacherous.

"It's a body all right," Philip said, when they were about five yards away. "A bloke."

"Is he dead, Phil?"

"Of course he's dead."

"I'm not going any closer."

" 'Aven't you never seen a dead body before?"

"No. 've you?"

"Lots."

It did strike Terry as odd that his friend had never disclosed this interesting detail before, but he decided to let it pass for the moment.

The body was lying spreadeagled on the mud, face down. One arm was outflung with the palm of the hand upwards, the other lay closer to his side.

Picking his way carefully forward, Philip reached the body and peered at it while Terry watched him anxiously from a safer distance. He saw his friend bend down and lift up one of the legs by the end of the trousers, dropping it again almost immediately.

"His hand's all white and wrinkled," Philip announced as he returned to Terry's side, "Like if you stay in the bath too long. My mum's hand went like that once when she went to sleep in the bath."

To Terry who detested baths as much as a cat, it was inconceivable that anyone could actually go to sleep in one.

"What did his face look like, Phil?"

"Kind of puffy what I could see of it."

"What sort of bloke is he?"

"Just an ordinary bloke."

"Why'd you pick up his leg?"

"Just to make sure 'e was dead," Philip said importantly.

"What are we going to do?"

" 'Ave to tell the police."

Terry nodded. "Let's go now, Phil. It's got creepy with 'im there."

"You go and I'll keep guard."

"Why've you got to do that? Why can't we go together?" There was a faint note of desperation in Terry's voice.

"Oh, all right!" Philip said gruffly and led the way to the foot of the ladder. "But we must hurry. Once the tide begins to turn, he'll float away. And who's going to believe us then?"

"They'll have to believe us. We found him." Terry paused. "I wonder if there'll be a reward, Phil?"

"If there is, we'll share it, of course."

They had reached the top of the ladder and set off across the rough ground at a trot.

They had barely squeezed through a gap in the surrounding fence when a police car came cruising toward them.

It came to a halt as they waved frantically at it. The driver wound down his window and gave them a suspicious look.

"What've you boys been up to?"

"We've found a dead bloke," Philip said while Terry nodded vigorously. "You'd better come quick or 'e'll be off."

The officer's expression registered yet greater suspicion.

"It's a serious matter wasting police time," he said sternly.

"We'll show you where it is," Terry said, gesticulating excitedly, "then you'll 'ave to believe us. But if you don't come quick it could float away."

The driver had a quick word with his colleague in the front passenger seat before getting out.

"Show me," he said in a tone which implied swift retribution should they be playing tricks.

It was fifteen minutes before the three of them returned to the police car. Sticking his head through the window, the driver said, "They're right. There is a body there. Get a message back." Turning to the boys, he added, "Hop in the back of the car you two."

When they were in, Terry gave Philip a nudge and whispered, "It's better than that time I cut my leg and went in an ambulance."

It was about six hours later that Detective Chief Inspector Pitcher found himself staring at the body which now lay naked on a mortuary slab.

The face was faintly bloated and the washer-woman hands indicated a lengthy immersion in water. He noticed that the skin of the lower abdomen had a greenish tinge.

"I'd say he'd been in the water about a couple of days," said Professor Wilding who had just performed an autopsy. "Further tests on various organs will be necessary if you require something more detailed. I take it you probably do."

Pitcher shook his head in a bemused way. "I'm not sure what part if any his death has in my murder case."

The pathologist frowned. "I thought he was someone you'd been looking for?"

"He is, but with less zeal since Frensham was charged. Nevertheless, I'd still have liked to have asked him a few questions."

"There's nothing to stop you *asking*," the pathologist remarked.

"I take it there's no doubt he died from drowning?"

"None at all."

"How'd he get into the water is what I'd like to know."

"Suicide or accident you mean?"

"Or murder."

"Murder! No one had told me that was a possibility." He bent over the corpse and gazed at it intently, occasionally stretching an area of skin or lifting a limb for closer examination. "I'd better resect the scalp and see if there's any subdural damage. Turn him over on to his face."

He seized a pair of clippers from the tray of instruments at his side and crudely cut away the hair from the back of the dead man's head. "I'm afraid I'd never be any good at sheep-shearing," he observed cheerfully.

He ran the tips of his fingers over the area of scalp from which the hair had just been removed and said thoughtfully:

"I think there is some bruising here. Where's our friend with the camera?"

The photographer stepped forward and took a number of shots as indicated by the pathologist.

"We'll take a look at the underside."

He made two deft strokes with a scalpel and peeled back a portion of scalp itself.

"Doesn't seem to be any fracture of the skull, but there's definitely evidence that he received a bang of sorts on the back of his head." He looked across at Pitcher. "Of course, it could have happened after he entered the water and was still alive. He could have banged his head against the column of a bridge or a boat for that matter."

"Or been hit and stunned before being thrown into the water?" Pitcher enquired.

"That's perfectly possible, too. At the moment I can't exclude any of those suggestions. I'll have to make a microscopic examination of the scalp tissue and the underlying bone before I can be more specific." He stood back and peeled off the gloves he had been wearing. "It's lucky you mentioned murder. I'd gathered it was just a straightforward case of drowning. I wouldn't have bothered with his head if you'd not alerted me."

"I don't know that he was murdered," Pitcher said helplessly. "I just wish I knew a bit more about him and what he's been up to the past few weeks. Then I might know whether he was murdered, threw himself into the river in a fit of depression or fell in when in a drunken stupor."

"With luck, I should be able to answer some of your questions, but it'll take a bit of time to do all the necessary tests. Like making a good casserole, you can't hurry the job."

"While you're doing that, I'll get in touch with the various river pundits and see if they can tell me where he was likely to have entered the water."

Professor Wilding walked across to a washbasin in the corner of the room.

"By the way," he said over his shoulder, "what's the fellow's name? I don't think anyone told me."

"Derek Unsworth," Pitcher replied.

He reflected that it was a rum job where you could slice someone open from neck to crutch, peel off their scalp and peer inside their head, all without bothering to know their name.

As he drove away from the mortuary, Pitcher felt that he could have done without Unsworth's intrusion on the scene as a corpse just two days before the hearing against Paul Frensham began. However his death had come about, it could only be an unwanted complicating factor. Or looked at another way, a further red herring for the defence to conjure with.

Clare first learnt of Unsworth's death when Nick came into the kitchen the next morning brandishing a newspaper.

"Listen to this," he said, and read out the item in question.

"Does it say how he died?" Clare asked.

"By drowning."

"I know. But how he came to be in the water?"

"Doesn't say." He threw the paper down on the table. "Presumably we shall now never find out what his row with Mrs. Isaacs was about."

But Clare appeared lost in deep thought and made no reply.

Chapter 21

"Is she here?"

Jim Jude was scarcely through the door of Pitcher's office before he put the question. He had come straight to the police station for a last-minute conference with Pitcher before the court hearing began.

Pitcher shook his head gloomily. " 'Fraid not. I phoned her again yesterday afternoon and reminded her of her promise to come back and how vital it was that we had her evidence, but she said she was unwell and couldn't travel."

"We don't believe that, do we?"

"All I can say, sir, is that she did manage to sound genuinely sorry that she was letting us down."

"That's no help. It's her testimony we want, not her regrets. She's obviously been warned to stay away by Sir Guy Frensham."

"I agree, sir, but we shall never be able to prove it and even if we could, is it any offence to persuade a foreigner not to return to this country to give evidence?"

"If it's not, it should be," Sergeant Lyle broke in. "If we had the evidence, I'd charge him and argue the toss afterwards."

"She gave no hint that the Frenshams had put pressure on her," Pitcher remarked. "She just kept on saying she hadn't been well and was unable to travel. She did add at the end that she'd be writing me a letter."

Lyle snorted as Jim Jude asked, "What about?"

"She didn't say."

"Well, we'll have to soldier on without her. If we manage to get the case past the magistrates, maybe she'll come over for the trial."

"Surely we've got a prima facie case on the scientific evidence alone?"

"Depends how it looks at the end. Anyway, I shall open the case in a low key. It's not one for opening high and then watching the scenery steadily collapse around you." He dropped his brief case on to a chair. "What are the latest developments over Unsworth's death?"

"I'm afraid there's nothing to add to what I told you on the phone yesterday," Pitcher replied. "He definitely died of drowning but, as you know we've no idea how he got into the water. We're making intensive enquiries of people who live up river to find out if anyone can throw any light on his death. We've put out appeals via the B.B.C. and the press for anyone who can give any information at all to contact the police and we've set up an incidents room in the area."

"Have you not been able to get an idea of where he entered the water?"

Pitcher shook his head. "At the moment, it could have been anywhere from one to five miles upstream. It's possible that an analysis of the water taken from his lungs may indicate a particular part of the river, but that won't be known for several days. And even then it's not a certainty."

"I'm surprised to learn that they can distinguish between one foully polluted stretch and another. But that apart, no one's yet come forward?"

"Only the inevitable cranks. One old lady phoned to tell us that her husband was drowned while bathing at Southend forty years ago and she wondered if it might be his body we'd found. Another denounced us for allowing bodies to get into the river, rather as though they were cars parking on double yellow lines."

Jude sighed. "I must say that Unsworth couldn't have chosen a less auspicious time or manner in which to turn up. He might at least have waited until the hearing before the magistrates was over."

A silence fell before Pitcher said, "Would you like a cup of coffee before we go to court?"

"That sounds like the best suggestion yet."

Twenty minutes later, they entered the Court building. As they thrust their way through the inevitable throng of people in the lobby, Pitcher nodded in the direction of one of the doors.

"That's Frensham over there."

His father and counsel and solicitor were standing protectively around him like supporters of a young hopeful about to enter the ring.

"Well, at least *he's* turned up," Jude remarked.

They passed into court where Jude got out his papers and settled back in his seat in readiness for the case to be called on. Shortly afterwards the defence team came in and Mr. Croxley took his place in the same row as Jude, but leaving a marked gap between them.

He leaned sideways to address Jude.

"Have we met before? My name's Warren Croxley."

"James Jude."

"As you'll be aware, we're contesting this case all the way, so I'll be glad if you'll refrain from leading the witnesses. Everything will be in issue."

"So I gather. Incidentally, one of my witnesses is unable to be here."

"Who's that?"

"Kerstin Borg. I thought you might know."

Mr. Croxley frowned disdainfully as though prosecuting Counsel had made a particularly tasteless remark and edged further away.

A few seconds later, Mr. Newsome, the clerk of the Court, entered and took his seat. He nodded pleasantly at Jude and cast Mr. Croxley a look of fervent dislike.

Shortly afterwards silence was called for and everyone in court rose as Mrs. Dowell and her two colleagues assumed their places on the bench.

Mr. Newsome made a sign to the jailer who tapped Paul Frensham on the arm and indicated he should step into the dock.

Mr. Croxley rose quickly and then waited until he had attracted everyone's attention.

"I have an application to make, your worships. It is that my client be allowed to sit immediately behind me and beside my instructing solicitor, as this will facilitate my conduct of the case and avoid movement every time I or Mr. Woodside need to speak to him. He appears here today in answer to his bail and I hope that no one"—at this point he glared at Mr. Newsome—"will suggest he is likely to flee the court if you permit this indulgence."

"Very well," Mrs. Dowell said, "we are prepared to allow that."

From her place in the front row of the public gallery, Clare watched Paul Frensham step out of the dock and sit beside his solicitor. From his expression, he'd have preferred to remain where he was.

Somewhere outside court Nick was restlessly waiting to give evidence, but Clare tried not to let thoughts of him distract her from listening to what was about to take place in court.

Jim Jude had told Pitcher that he proposed to open the case for the prosecution in a low key and this he now proceeded to do. He stressed that the most damning evidence against the accused was that which would be coming from the laboratory witness, who would tell the court not only of the thorough washing of the sweater, but of the green earring found beside the dead woman which had fibres from the sweater adhering to it. With the defection of Kerstin Borg, he was denied being able to mention that she had given the accused the earring and that he had worn it on his sweater. If he felt frustrated, he showed no signs of it as he unfolded the story which would shortly be supported by the evidence of his witnesses.

"The prosecution's duty, madam," he said, addressing Mrs. Dowell and her colleagues, "is to satisfy you of a prima facie case; that is, of evidence on which a jury acting reasonably could convict. Not will or should, but could. In these days of formal committals for trial, it is rare for you to be called upon to exercise your erstwhile function as examining magistrates, hearing all the evidence live and deciding whether it constitutes a case to answer. At this stage, the prosecution will do no more than suggest that if you accept the scientific evidence and if you are satisfied that the accused was wearing that sweater at Mrs. Isaacs' house on the afternoon in question, then you may well consider that he has a case to answer in the Crown court."

"If there is a case, it will be very fully answered in this court," Mr. Croxley said in a thick gravy rumble.

The first two witnesses were respectively a civilian photographer from the photographic section at Scotland Yard and a police constable who had prepared a scale plan of 14 Teeling Road.

Their evidence was formal and non-controversial, though this did not stop Mr. Croxley from cross-examining each of them at some length, to the apparent exasperation of Mr. Newsome.

"Is it necessary," he asked, after he could keep silent no longer, "to get the witness to describe what is perfectly clear in the photographs themselves?"

"I will conduct my cross-examination as I see fit," Mr. Croxley replied with hauteur.

"As long as you're not expecting it all to be recorded in the witness' deposition?"

"If the deposition is not a faithful record of the witness' evidence I shall, of course, make my objection."

For a few seconds the two men exchanged sulphurous looks and then defending counsel resumed his questions, while the clerk who had been recording the evidence on tape, lay down the microphone as if suddenly called out on strike.

A tactful intervention by Mrs. Dowell resolved the impasse and the case continued.

Clare reckoned that, at this rate, it could last for days, which meant she would have to make further arrangements for Simon's care. Having overcome Nick's scruples and gotten herself to court, she intended seeing the case through to its end.

Jude's first witness of substance was Professor Hightree who had performed the autopsy on Mrs. Isaacs; not that his evidence seemed likely to give rise to controversy.

He gave her cause of death as multiple fractures of the skull and said that her injuries were consistent with having been caused by a cast-iron replica of a King Charles spaniel, which he had observed when he visited the scene of the crime and which had blood and head hairs adhering to it.

"Would you say that this was a frenzied attack?" Mr. Croxley asked when he rose to cross-examine.

The witness smiled thinly. "It's a question of terminology, I suppose. I'd prefer to say vicious rather than frenzied."

"How many blows were struck to cause the injuries you've described?"

"I'd say at least three or four."

"Three or four vicious blows?"

"They were certainly severe."

"You said vicious just now."

"They were severe blows, delivered, in my opinion, with a good deal of viciousness."

"If you please," Mr. Croxley said in a throaty purr, "would any one of the blows have been sufficient to cause death?"

"Very probably."

"I am much obliged for that answer."

"The witness is not giving evidence in order to oblige you," Mr.

144

Newsome broke in. "Comments of that nature do not assist the court."

"Please go on," Mrs. Dowell said hurriedly.

Mr. Croxley who had been on the point of making a riposte gave her an understanding nod which contrived to convey his sympathy to the bench for having such an obnoxious clerk. He turned his attention back to the witness.

"Do you really disagree with the word frenzied?" he asked in his most oleaginous tone.

Professor Hightree shrugged. "I don't think I can add to what I said earlier."

"So you do disagree?" Mr. Newsome put in briskly.

"It's certainly not the word of my choice."

"Any further questions to ask this witness?" the clerk demanded.

Mr. Croxley, who had been on the point of resuming his seat, immediately straightened up.

"I'd like to know whether you found any other injuries on the body of the deceased?"

"I did not."

"She had been attacked from behind?"

"He said that," the clerk remarked.

"I have no further questions, your worship," Mr. Croxley said, giving Mrs. Dowell a small gratuitous bow.

Jude rose. "I have called Professor Hightree out of sequence as he is required in another court, and I shall be grateful if he may now be released?"

Mrs. Dowell glanced toward Mr. Croxley who added his agreement.

The next witness was Oliver Gill, who came into court wearing fawn slacks, a blue blazer and a black knitted tie. Clare watched him with interest. He took the oath in a nervous voice and then fixed his gaze on Jude who was waiting to question him.

He agreed that he had attended the mortuary where he had identified a body as that of his aunt, Florence Isaacs. He said he had last seen her about a week before her death and had been accustomed to visit her once a month or so.

It wasn't part of Jude's case to probe their relationship and he contented himself with eliciting one or two domestic and family details such as that she lived alone at 14 Teeling Road and that he was her only surviving relative.

Gill's attitude in the box seemed to be one of eagerness to please everyone. After every answer he would look quickly around the court as though seeking approbation. And then he would grip the ledge in front of him as he awaited the next question. From time to time, he would put a hand up to smooth his unruffled, if thinning, head of fair hair.

Jude's final question to him concerned the green earring found beside his aunt's body. It was passed up to him by the exhibits officer.

"Can you say whether or not that was your aunt's earring?"

"I never saw her wear it," he said, with an ingratiating smile. "Indeed, it doesn't bear comparison with any of her other jewellery. To answer your question, sir, I'd say it's not hers."

Jude sat down and Mr. Croxley unfolded himself and faced the witness like a boa constrictor sizing up its next meal.

"Were you fond of your aunt, Mr. Gill?" he asked in a judicious voice.

Gill blinked at him. "Of course, she was my only relative."

"It doesn't follow that you had to be fond of her."

"I suppose not."

"So were you?"

"I had a feeling of duty toward her."

"That's quite a different matter, though most commendable if I may say so. Is it not a fact, Mr. Gill, that she was a rather difficult old lady?"

"I suppose you could say so."

"A bit cantankerous?"

"Well, yes, she could be."

"Rather fond of complaining?"

Gill allowed himself a wispy smile. "Yes, she was rather full of complaints at times."

Mr. Croxley turned a beaming expression on the witness. "I expect that even you were sometimes the object of unmerited complaint?"

"Yes, that's true."

"Would you describe her as a lonely old lady?"

"I don't think she ever felt really lonely."

"Friendless, then?"

"She certainly didn't have many friends."

"I don't want to beat about the bush, Mr. Gill, but would I not be right in describing the deceased as a quarrelsome old lady?"

Clare leaned forward intently as Gill appeared to deliberate his answer with a faint frown.

"Yes, I'm afraid she was rather quarrelsome."

"Quarrelsome and complaining?"

"Yes, in fact she quite often complained about your client." The answer was accompanied by a small apologetic smile.

"About the quality of his work as a gardener, you mean?" Mr. Croxley said sharply.

"Yes, she found him unsatisfactory and was thinking of dismissing him."

"Let us not get this out of perspective," defending counsel said in a severe tone. "You're not suggesting, are you, that my client stood alone in her estimation as an object of criticism?"

Gill appeared taken aback by Mr. Croxley's abrupt change of tone and was anxious to make amends.

"Oh, certainly not," he said in a placatory voice. "Why the last time I saw her she complained bitterly about her new window cleaner who'd failed to start when he'd promised."

"Quite so," Mr. Croxley said, mollified. "Almost everyone who came into contact with her was the object of complaint, that's so, isn't it?" He glanced up when Gill didn't immediately answer and said sharply, "Well, isn't it?"

To Clare, the witness had a suddenly distracted expression. It was as though he had remembered leaving something baking in the oven and was wondering if his home had by now been burnt to the ground.

Brought back to reality by the sharpness of Mr. Croxley's tone, Gill now gave a vacant nod.

"I want to ask you some questions about a man named Derek Unsworth. You know whom I'm referring to?"

Again Gill nodded, seemingly more as a reflex than as a positive response.

"You must answer yes or no," Mr. Newsome broke in. "I can't record nods."

"I'm sorry. Yes, I did meet Unsworth two or three times."

"He lived in a flat at the top of your aunt's house?"

"Yes."

"But after two months, he left abruptly?"

"Yes."

"Why?"

"I don't know the reason."

"Is it not true that he and your aunt had a row?"

"I believe so."

"What was the row about?"

"I've no idea."

"Your aunt didn't tell you?"

"No, she was very secretive about it."

Mr. Newsome who had been looking increasingly restive for several minutes now broke in. "Does this line of cross-examination have any relevance?"

"Most certainly it does."

"What?"

"It shows that the deceased was a difficult, quarrelsome old lady who by her behaviour had become the object of general ill-will on the part of those who had contact with her." Mr. Croxley now lifted his eyes from the top of the clerk's head, which he had been addressing, to Mrs. Dowell. "I am sure your worships will have appreciated the great relevance of my line of cross-examination. And now if I may be allowed to continue . . ." Mr. Newsome let out a heavy sigh, but no one spoke and Mr. Croxley turned his attention back to the witness. "I was asking you about Mr. Unsworth before that interruption. Until his abrupt and mysterious departure from your aunt's house, had he always seemed to be on very good terms with her?"

"Yes."

"You know, of course, that he has been found drowned within the last forty-eight hours?"

"The Police have told me. And I'd also read it in the paper."

"Having left your aunt's house after a furious row?"

"Is that meant to be a question?" Mr. Newsome enquired acidly.

"It is a question."

"I think their worships would regard it more as a comment."

Mrs. Dowell nodded her agreement and Mr. Croxley gave a petulant shrug.

"Was your aunt afraid of Unsworth after their row?"

"She didn't say so."

"But she could have been?"

This time it was Mrs. Dowell who intervened. "I don't think the witness can answer that question, Mr. Croxley."

"Very well, I won't pursue it," defending counsel said in a lofty tone, and sat down.

It appeared to Clare that Gill showed considerable relief when he realised that his questioning had reached an end. She watched him as he stepped down from the witness box and made his way to a seat at the back of the court. She saw him take a handkerchief from his pocket and wipe his forehead. She was still thinking about the evidence he had given when his place in the box was taken by Mrs.

Rawlings who took the oath and glanced about her with an expression of strong disapproval.

Her head scarf was knotted so tightly beneath her chin that her cheeks bulged out as though inflated by a tyre pump.

Jude who had had long experience of eliciting evidence from witnesses of every age and from every walk of life knew that the one thing they all had in common was nerves. Rare indeed was the witness who, whatever his outward mien, did not feel nervous on going into the box. He quickly realised that Mrs. Rawlings was shaking with nerves behind her formidable expression of disapproval.

"Mrs. Rawlings," he said with a friendly smile, "I have very few questions to ask you and I hope they won't cause you too much distress."

While he was speaking, Mrs. Rawlings maintained a wary eye on him and continued to do so while she answered his questions about the discovery of Mrs. Isaacs' body.

At one point he prefaced a question with, "I'm sorry to have to ask you about such grisly details," only to have the witness say in a tone of undisguised scorn, "When you've lived as long as me, there's nowt special about a dead body." There was a faint titter of laughter at the back of the court until quelled by a glare from the witness herself.

When Mr. Croxley rose to cross-examine, she fixed him with the same look of frowning suspicion.

"I gather you didn't much care for your employer, Mrs. Rawlings?" Mr. Croxley said in a hearty voice.

"I keeps myself to myself."

"Yes, but is it right that you didn't like Mrs. Isaacs?"

"Who says I didn't?" Mrs. Rawlings' tone was indignant.

"Did you or didn't you?"

"What've my likes or dislikes got to do with it?"

Mr. Newsome smiled complacently, as Mrs. Dowell said, "Defending counsel is only doing his job, Mrs. Rawlings. If you could just try and answer his questions. . . ."

"She 'ad 'er ways and I 'ave mine. I did what I was paid to do and didn't take a lot of notice of 'er."

"Would you agree that she was a difficult woman to get on with?"

"No more'n some."

Mr. Croxley pursed his lips and appeared undecided whether to do further battle with her. His instructions informed him that the witness had never been well-disposed toward his client and this meant that further cross-examination on these lines would run the risk of getting unfavourable answers. Her evidence hadn't touched Paul Frensham but, at the same time, it was clear she wasn't going to throw anything his way. Discretion won and Mr. Croxley sat down.

This was much to Clare's chagrin as she had been hoping to see the redoubtable Mrs. Rawlings wipe the floor with defending counsel.

The next witness to be called was Betsy, Alice Macpherson's friend. At first Clare couldn't think what evidence she had to give. It soon transpired, however, that she was being called to fill in a blank created by Kerstin Borg's defection.

Under Jude's direction, she was shown the green earring and said that it was identical with a pair possessed by Kersty, the other one of which was red.

"And who is Kersty?" Jude asked.

"Kerstin Borg. She worked as an au pair at Sir Guy and Lady Frensham's."

"I take it she is not being called?" Mr. Newsome asked with one eyebrow quizzically raised.

"She's returned to Sweden," Jude replied.

"And is confined to her sick bed," Mr. Croxley added in a loud aside. "Tell the court that."

In an elaborately dry tone, Jude said, "The prosecution had wished to call Miss Borg as a witness but she is not available for the reason you've heard. She returned to her home in Sweden a short time ago and my latest information, confirmed by my learned friend's interjection, is that she is unwell and not able to travel."

It seemed to Clare that, apart from Paul Frensham who was slightly smirking, the remainder of the defence team, including Sir Guy himself, wore expressions of matching stoniness as this information was imparted to the court.

Immediately afterwards Mr. Croxley rose to cross-examine and fixed the witness with a stern look.

"You can't possibly swear on oath that the green earring you've been shown is Miss Borg's, can you?"

"It looks like hers."

"Maybe it does, but only because there are a thousand others of identical design. That's so, isn't it?"

"I can only say that I've never seen another pair like them," Betsy said sweetly and added, "They're not English you know. They're Danish."

"I don't mind where they come from," Mr. Croxley observed tartly. "They're obviously mass-produced."

150

"We have no evidence to that effect," Mr. Newsome purred. "Only what this witness has said about them."

"Evidence will be forthcoming," Mr. Croxley retorted and quickly sat down.

After a short, whispered conversation with her two colleagues and Mr. Newsome, Mrs. Dowell announced that the court would adjourn until two o'clock.

As Clare pushed her way through a throng of people round the exit, she noticed Alice Macpherson running up the steps outside the building. A second later, Alice spotted her and came across.

"Has Betsy given evidence yet?"

"She's just finished."

"Oh, dear. I promised to be here, but I got held up. Was she all right?"

"Fine."

"We'd arranged to have lunch together, why don't you join us?" Then she quickly added, "But of course, you'll be having lunch with Nick."

Clare shook her head. "No, I'm not. He's been out of court waiting to give his evidence and it would look bad if we were seen together. The defence might suggest that I'd been priming him and that could make things even worse than they are. Anyway, we agreed that we oughtn't to be seen together even after he's given his evidence. You're about the only person here who knows me and it's probably better that way."

"Well, let's find Betsy and go off to lunch," Alice said, looking about her. "There she is, over on the pavement."

Clare, who had not been looking forward to a lonely sandwich and her own morbid company, was delighted to join the other two girls. It was toward the end of their frugal meal that Alice enquired how soon Nick would be giving his evidence.

"I don't really know, but he could be next."

"Would you like me to come into court with you?" Clare gave a grateful nod. "It won't embarrass you?"

"No, I'd love to have a sympathetic person beside me. I'm not sure which of us will be suffering the more, Nick or me."

"But you still want to be there?" Alice said in a slightly puzzled tone.

"Yes, I may be able to notice things which Nick misses. Things that could affect the outcome of his suspension. There've been one or two things already."

Alice waited for her to go on, but when Clare didn't she suggested they should get their bill and return to court.

As they arrived back outside the building, a chauffeur-driven Mercedes pulled up and disgorged Sir Guy Frensham and Paul together with Mr. Croxley and Mr. Woodside.

Clare squeezed up to make room for Alice in their already crowded row. As she glanced around the courtroom, she noticed three additional occupants in the police seats. For a second, she wondered who they were and then sudden realisation made her mouth go dry and her throat hurt. The tall, professorial-looking one was obviously Detective Chief Superintendent Upperton, next to him was his sidekick and immediately behind them, recognisable by her notebook, was a shorthand-writer.

So a close examination of Nick's evidence today was to be part of Upperton's enquiry! Clare felt herself burning with resentment. As if his ordeal wasn't sufficient without seeing this dispassionate trio weighing his every word and assessing every flicker of expression.

A few minutes later, the hearing resumed and Jude announced that his next witness was Detective Sergeant Attwell.

Clare watched Nick come in through the door at the back of the court and walk briskly toward the witness box. He missed his footing as he reached the three steps that led up to the box and stumbled forward but quickly recovered himself. Not, however, before Clare's heart had skipped a beat. She might have been watching him teeter on a precipice.

He took the oath in a firm voice and turned to face Jude, who began by eliciting his name and rank.

"Is it a fact, Sergeant Attwell," Jude went on, "that you are at present suspended from duty as a result of an allegation of attempted bribery made against you by the accused in this case?"

"Yes, sir."

In Jude's experience, it was always better for the prosecution to remove as much of the sting in such a situation as it could and so neutralise some of the defence histrionics in advance.

"Did you in fact solicit a bribe from the accused at any stage of your dealings with him?"

"I did not, sir."

Nick went on to describe his going to the Frensham house and Paul later accompanying him to the police station.

In answer to Jude's question, he told of his taking possession of the recently washed sweater.

"Did you notice anything in particular while you were in the accused's bedroom?"

"Yes, sir. Among various odds and ends on his dressing table was a small red object."

"What sort of object?"

"At the time, sir, I didn't give it a great deal of attention. It struck me as being a button of sorts."

"Did you take possession of it?"

Nick shook his head unhappily. "No, sir. It didn't strike me as significant then."

Jude nodded and asked that Nick be shown the green earring. "Was the red object anything like that, apart from colour?"

"Yes, sir, it's front was identical in shape and size. I can't, of course, say whether it had a similar clasp on the back as I never touched it."

Jude gave a satisfied nod and sat down.

Clare clenched her muscles as Mr. Croxley rose to cross-examine.

"Am I right in thinking that an officer is not *automatically* suspended as a result of an allegation of corruption made against him by a member of the public?"

"Yes, sir."

"But *you* have been suspended?"

"Yes."

"Do you know why?"

"I think so."

"Would it be because the allegation is true?"

"No, because it isn't true, sir."

"But you were immediately suspended?"

"Yes, I've already said so."

"Doesn't this indicate that your superiors have little faith in your denial of the allegation?"

Jude jumped to his feet. "That is not a question the witness can answer."

"I agree," Mr. Newsome said.

"Let me put it this way, then," Mr. Croxley went on. "Do you accept that your superiors cast grave doubt on your credibility as a witness?"

"I do not," Nick replied hotly at the same moment as Mr. Newsome intervened once more.

"The witness' credibility is a matter for the court to assess," he said.

Mr. Croxley who knew this quite well merely blinked at the ceiling.

"This red object you say you saw is pure invention on your part, isn't it?"

"No. I definitely did see it."

"But it was so unimportant to you at the time you just left it there?"

"Yes, I've explained that."

"When, according to your story, did you suddenly appreciate its significance?"

"When I began to think about the lone green one which had been found at the scene. It just didn't seem to be the sort of thing an old person like Mrs. Isaacs would wear."

"You're just making your evidence up as we go along, aren't you?" Mr. Croxley said in a sarcastic drawl.

"Certainly not."

"Is it because you feel your position is so bad that perjury can't make it worse?"

Clare felt a restraining hand on her arm and sat back, giving Alice a fleetingly wan smile.

Meanwhile Jude was again on his feet. "That, madam," he said addressing Mrs. Dowell, "is not a question but a comment; and a most improper comment at that."

"Yes, please confine yourself to questions, Mr. Croxley," the chairman said.

"I'm sorry, your worship, if I let my indignation run away with me," Mr. Croxley replied in an unrepentant tone. He returned his attention to Nick who was staring straight ahead of him with a masked expression.

"Would you agree, officer, that your whole attitude toward my client was that of a bully?"

"No, sir."

"You pushed your way into the house?"

"He didn't try and stop me entering."

"And later overrode his protests in searching his bedroom?"

"I had a right, sir, to look for and take possession of anything of evidential significance once I was in the house."

"Oh, yes, I know the law, too," Mr. Croxley said in a sarcastic voice. "It was your entry that was unlawful. That's right, isn't it?"

"No, sir. The accused allowed me to enter."

"Because of your bullying manner?"

"No."

"And then later when you drove him to the police station, you asked him for two thousand pounds to suppress an important clue?"

"That's quite incorrect, sir. I did nothing of the sort."

"Was the important clue this red earring?"

"I didn't realise it was important then, as I've explained. It was only later."

"I suggest, officer, that you invented the red earring in order to garnish the case against my client after he had turned you down over the bribe you attempted to obtain?"

"That's a complete travesty of the truth," Nick said vehemently. He seemed about to go on, but quickly bit his lip and said no more.

The truth was that, since his interview with Upperton at Scotland Yard, he had been haunted by the fact that his evidence about seeing the red earring tended to support Frensham's allegation of corruption. He now felt certain that Frensham, having realised the earring had been spotted and might subsequently become associated with the green one found at the scene of the crime, decided to make his allegation for the sole purpose of diminishing the effect of the very evidence Nick had just given. Discredit the witness before he even appreciates what he can say!

Clare knew what was going through his mind as she watched him standing tensely in the box. They had discussed the dilemma countless times over the past week. By giving his evidence, Nick would be adding weight to Paul Frensham's allegation and also laying himself open to the further suggestion that he'd invented it in order to enhance the prospect of Frensham's conviction. His hope had rested uneasily on Kerstin Borg. She alone could corroborate what he'd said. It had been a shattering blow to learn that she wouldn't be giving evidence.

Clare found herself looking at Sir Guy Frensham with loathing. This man who pretended to be the public protector of the unprotected, but who didn't scruple when his own personal life was affected to use his money and influence to ensure a miscarriage of justice.

"I put it to you, officer," Mr. Croxley now went on, the corners of his mouth turned down in an expression of distaste, "that your evidence concerning my client is a tissue of lies from beginning to end?"

"I've told the truth, sir."

Defending counsel held up an imperious hand. "And that you are both a corrupt and a perjurous police officer?"

"I am neither and your client knows it," Nick said, leaning forward and glaring at Paul Frensham who was sitting with a smug expression on his face.

Clare felt herself go suddenly limp. It was as though she'd just survived a particularly scary ride on the big dipper, which had seemed without end. She was aware of Alice studying her anxiously and she gave her friend a small nod of reassurance. She didn't know whether Nick had recognised Alice beside her. Probably not as he had studiously refrained from looking around the courtroom. But she didn't mind if he had seen the two of them together. She was now ready to tell him of her involvement.

She forced her attention back to Jude who was telling the court that as Mr. Broughton, the witness from the laboratory, was still giving evidence in another court, he proposed to call Detective Chief Inspector Pitcher out of normal order.

The officer in charge of a case, even though a witness, is usually allowed to stay in court in order to assist prosecuting counsel with any points arising suddenly in the course of the hearing. Mr. Croxley, however, had insisted on his right to have *all* the prosecution witnesses out of court while waiting to give evidence.

In answer to Jude's questions, Pitcher described how he'd attended the scene of the crime and observed the body of the deceased lying on her bedroom floor. He went on to testify about his interview with Paul Frensham and of his having been present when he was charged with murder.

As she listened to him, Clare thought he sounded as nice as she'd imagined him to be. He seemed to belong to that breed of police officer who kept an open mind and didn't necessarily go along with the popular view. She saw him as somebody who'd not be afraid to express a minority opinion against some of the accepted police prejudices, most of which revolved round the belief that the criminal law had become soft and made things too easy for the crooks.

He gazed calmly at Mr. Croxley as he rose to cross-examine.

"Tell me, officer, did you ever suspect this man Unsworth of the murder?" Defending counsel's voice assumed a faintly hectoring note.

"I certainly wished to interview him, sir."

"Because of his abrupt departure from Mrs. Isaacs' house following a mysterious row?"

"Correct."

"You wanted to find out what the row was about?"

"Yes."

"Because it might have had something to do with her death?"

"It might have."

156

"But Unsworth had disappeared and you were unable to trace him?"

"That's correct."

"Until he was fished out of the Thames two days ago?"

"Yes."

"Very mystifying, isn't it, officer?"

"It's certainly left a number of questions unanswered."

"Exactly," Mr. Croxley observed with a vigorous nod. "Is it not a possibility that Unsworth drowned himself in a fit of remorse after killing the old lady who'd befriended him?"

Pitcher appeared to cogitate his answer. "I suppose anything is possible, sir," he said slowly, "but there's no evidence to that effect."

"But it makes sense, doesn't it, officer?"

"Until we know more about the circumstances of Unsworth's drowning, I don't think I can answer that, sir."

"But you agree it's a possibility?"

"I can only repeat that I've found no evidence to support it."

"Somebody who actually lived in the deceased's house leaves suddenly after a mysterious row, then disappears and is later found drowned: are you denying that that whole sequence of events is fraught with significance?"

"It certainly leaves a number of questions unanswered, as I've already said, sir."

"Very unsatisfactory?"

"I agree."

"Let me now turn to something else. I think you know of a young man named Rivings? Anthony Rivings?"

"Yes, sir."

"Is he awaiting trial on a charge of burglary in relation to the deceased's house?"

"Yes."

"He's a young man with a criminal record?"

"Yes."

"For dishonesty?"

"Yes."

"Who is this Rivings?" Mr. Newsome broke in.

"He was a friend of the accused," Pitcher answered.

"Would you accept that he dominated my client?" Mr. Croxley asked.

"I've no evidence that he did."

"He was several years older?"

"Yes."

"Much bigger physically?"

"Yes."

"Did you never regard him as a suspect of the murder?"

"Not seriously."

"Did you or did you not ever regard him as a suspect?" Mr. Croxley asked in a tetchy voice.

"At the beginning of a murder enquiry, sir, it's not unusual for a whole range of people to come under suspicion until one by one they're eliminated."

"So you've eliminated Rivings?"

"Yes."

"But not Unsworth! You can't have eliminated Unsworth as a suspect?"

"I've already explained. . . ."

"Don't prevaricate, officer, I want an answer to my question."

"As I've said, I've no evidence. . . ."

"Officer," Mr. Croxley said in a stentorian tone, "answer my question."

"He keeps on answering it," Mr. Newsome remarked wearily.

Ignoring the interruption, Mr. Croxley continued to fix Pitcher with an imperious stare. "Well?"

"If Unsworth were alive, I'd certainly want to interview him," Pitcher replied.

"Before you could eliminate him as a suspect?"

"Yes, in a sense."

"Thank you, officer," Mr. Croxley said, adding, "At last!" as, rolling his eyes ceilingwards, he resumed his seat.

Shortly afterwards, the court adjourned for the day. Clare and Alice made their way out together. Nick was nowhere in sight.

For a while, the two girls stood on the steps of the courthouse. Alice was ready to leave, but Clare hung back and appeared to be deep in thought.

"Don't wait for me," Clare said when she became aware of her friend's restiveness.

A minute or two later, the opportunity presented itself. But even as Clare walked across to where he was standing alone, she was uncertain whether she was actually going to accost him.

"Excuse me, I'm Nick Attwell's wife," she heard herself say to him. "I'd like to talk to you, Mr. Pitcher."

Chapter 22

Clare was scarcely aware of the worn appearance of Pitcher's office, as she recounted her story, partly because such surroundings were familiar to her, but more particularly because her mind was so heavily concentrated on the task in hand.

He listened to her in silence, his expression never revealing his thoughts. Once or twice, Clare paused and waited for a reaction of some sort but none ever came and she would continue like a long-distance runner condemned to finish the course at whatever the cost.

When at last she finished, he gave a heavy sigh as if to convey that he wished she had never begun. For a time, he sat staring across the room, plucking at his lower lip while Clare watched him nervously. It was all she could do to prevent herself telling him to leave his face alone.

At length he turned his gaze on her. A gaze that was neither hostile nor friendly.

"It's pretty far-fetched, isn't it?" he said in a tone which seemed to seek reassurance.

Clare let out a silent sigh of relief. She'd been half-expecting a brush-off and possibly worse. A rebuke might yet come but at least he hadn't resorted to it as an excuse for ignoring her story.

"But it must be worth checking," she replied eagerly.

"It's not necessarily going to do Nick any good. You realise that?" Clare felt as if he had punched her in the face. He went on, "I confess I find it all a bit puzzling. You rush around making your own private enquiries, supposedly in the cause of clearing your husband's name and now you come and shovel the results on to my desk and expect me to finish what you've begun. Well, even if I do, I repeat that it's not necessarily going to help Nick. Get my point?"

Clare took a deep breath. "Of course everything I've done has been to help Nick. I've done it because I know he's innocent."

Pitcher looked unmoved. "It's the greatest pity you didn't let me know when you first traced Unsworth. That would have been far more helpful than all this private eye stuff."

His tone was scathing, but Clare was more than ever determined not to allow herself to be thrown on the defensive.

"But it still doesn't invalidate what I've told you."

"And what have you told me? A lot of surmise about a mysterious piece of paper hidden somewhere in the deceased's house which will explain her death. And added to that a further piece of even greater surmise. That's all it amounts to, isn't it?"

"Yes, but it can be very easily checked."

"Hmmm!" He began fingering his lower lip again and Clare's confidence grew. She had told him too much for it to be swept aside without investigation, however tempting it might be to let matters rest.

"You realise, Mrs. Attwell, that you're asking me to lift the lid off a Pandora's Box?"

Clare shook her head. "All I'm asking you to do is to investigate what I've told you. It was only as a result of what happened in court today that I knew the time had come when I must speak to you. I'm grateful to you for having listened to me. I accept your reproach about not having come to you before, but I am quite unrepentant about what I've done. Just as I'm sure your wife would be in similar circumstances."

There was a knock on the door and they both looked toward it. It opened to reveal Nick.

"I'm sorry to disturb you, sir, but I'm looking for my wife. I was told she was here." At this point, his eyes fell on Clare, who was partially hidden from his view.

"We've just completed our business, Nick," Pitcher observed. "She'll doubtless tell you about it on the way home."

Nick stared at his wife with a puzzled frown, but Clare avoided his look and walked across to the door. As soon as it was closed behind him, he turned on her angrily.

"I knew I shouldn't have let you come to court. What've you been seeing the guv'nor about? You've no right to talk to him behind my back."

Clare said nothing. In fact what she most wanted to do was put her arms round his neck and kiss him, but she decided she had better restrain the impulse.

For some time after Clare had left his office, Pitcher sat staring at the wall, feet propped on a corner of his desk. He had realised at an early stage that he would have to follow up what Clare had told him, whatever the consequences. His mood was one of resignation. If she was right, the consequences could be far-reaching. On the other hand, the whole thing could prove to be a damp firework.

All he hoped was that any further enquiries would reach a conclusion of some sort. That Clare's theory would be either proved or firmly disproved. He reached for the telephone.

"Get me Mr. Wystan. He'll probably be at home by now. I don't know his number but get him urgently." A couple of minutes later the phone rang and the officer on the switchboard told him that the bank manager was on the line. "I'm sorry to trouble you at home," Pitcher said, "but I want to make a further search of Mrs. Isaacs' house. Can someone meet me there with the keys? . . . Yes, this evening . . . Yes, I'm afraid it is urgent."

The bank was clearly not geared to muster a member of its staff after office hours and Pitcher chafed while he waited for the manager to call him back.

It was almost an hour later that he set off in his car to pick up a clerk named Colin Rowcliffe who, Mr. Wystan informed him, had been responsible for making an inventory of Mrs. Isaacs' effects. Mr. Wystan's tone when he rang back had indicated both his annoyance at the trouble he'd been put to and his relief at having been able to pass a tiresome chore to one of his junior clerks.

Pitcher was alone, having decided that for the time being he would keep Clare's information to himself. He found Colin Rowcliffe standing on the pavement outside the bank where he had had to go to collect the keys.

"I'm sorry to drag you out like this," Pitcher said as Rowcliffe got into the passenger seat beside him.

The young man grunted. "How long's it going to take? I'm meant to be taking my girl-friend to the pictures this evening."

"Not too long, I hope," Pitcher replied in a mollifying tone.

"I'm not exactly clear what it is you're looking for?"

"To be truthful nor am I."

Rowcliffe shot him a suspicious glance. "I only thought it might save time if you told me," he said in a huffed tone. "I've listed most of her property, including all the small items."

Pitcher sighed. "I'm looking for a piece of paper."

"A piece of paper!"

"Yes. Don't ask me what's on it because I don't know. It could be a letter or a note of some sort. Perhaps a more formal document. All I hope is that, if I find it, I'll recognise it for what it is."

"Are you sure it's there?"

"No."

"Good grief, it'll be worse than looking for a needle in a haystack."

"Very likely."

Rowcliffe lapsed into a gloomy silence, clearly seeing his prospect of an evening at the cinema rapidly receding.

After a pause, Pitcher went on, "I take it you've not come across anything of the sort in the course of your inventory?" Rowcliffe shook his head despondently. "Have you been through all her desk drawers?"

"Yes."

"Where would you hide a piece of paper you didn't wish to be found?" Pitcher's tone was cajoling.

Rowcliffe thought for a moment. "Depends how big it was. I'd probably hide it in my sock drawer or somewhere like that."

Pitcher nodded encouragingly. "But you've been through all her clothes drawers and not found anything?"

"Only bits of money. She has it tucked away everywhere."

Voicing Clare's own suggestion, Pitcher asked, "What about between the pages of a book?"

"I suppose that might be quite a good place, provided it wasn't a book in constant use."

"I seem to recall there was a set of some poet's work in the drawing-room."

"Yes, Tennyson."

"You've not examined each volume separately?"

"Didn't need to, there are twelve of them."

"Then that's where we'll begin."

Leaving the car out in the road, they walked up the short, dark drive to the front door. Taking a bunch of keys from his coat pocket, Rowcliffe selected one and a moment later they were in the hall. He turned on a light.

"Has an unlived-in smell, doesn't it?" Pitcher remarked, sniffing the air.

"It's spooky if you ask me. I wouldn't want to be here alone after dark."

"Well, let's get on." They entered the drawing-room. "Better pull the curtains."

While Rowcliffe was doing this, Pitcher walked across to the bookcase in which the row of paperback thrillers occupied the lower shelf and the set of white buckskin bound Tennyson the upper. The thrillers looked as well worn as the volumes of Tennyson looked untouched.

Selecting the first volume, Pitcher blew off a coating of dust and riffled through its pages.

Trying hard to suppress his impatience, Rowcliffe watched him work his way along the row.

The first seven volumes revealed nothing, not even Mrs. Isaacs' penchant for concealing money in unusual places.

The eighth volume he examined was entitled "Maud &" and was, if anything, dustier than the others. As Pitcher banged its covers together a folded sheet of paper fell out and fluttered to the floor. He bent down and picked it up. The crease of the paper was etched in dirt and its edges soiled.

All this he noticed with a sudden spurt of interest as he unfolded it and stared at the clear, bold writing which covered the page.

His eye flickered from "Dear Florence" at the top of the sheet to "Your affectionate sister, Dorothea" at the bottom; then back again to the top where a date appeared. It was "August 14th, 1944."

Slowly he read through the letter while Rowcliffe watched him with frowning impatience.

"Is that what you were looking for?" Rowcliffe asked, taking a hopeful step toward the door.

Pitcher nodded thoughtfully. "Yes . . . . it must be. I think it must be."

"Shall we go then?" Rowcliffe hovered at the door like a waiter trying to be rid of a last diner.

In silence they walked back to the car. As they were getting in,

Pitcher spoke for the first time since they'd left the house.
"Do you know where I can find the window cleaner?"
"Window cleaner?" Rowcliffe asked sharply.
"Yes, Mrs. Isaacs' window cleaner. The one who never came."

Chapter 23

Clare was forced to conclude that she didn't know her husband as well as she imagined. She had expected at least disapproval and most probably a much stronger reaction when she told him what she'd been up to. Instead he had slowly shaken his head in disbelief. Then he had said, "And to think I never had an inkling."

She was subsequently to reflect that perhaps his observation showed that he, for his part, didn't know his wife as well as he might have.

"The guv'nor can't have been too pleased," he added. Clare shrugged as though Pitcher's reaction was not her responsibility. "You're pretty confident, aren't you?" he went on, looking at her with a fond expression.

"I wish I could be more confident that what I've done is going to help you." She bit her lip. "After all, that's the only reason I did it. I wasn't just trying to be clever."

Nick pulled her toward him and kissed her. "I know you only did it for me and I love you for it. Whatever the result."

Clare gave a small shiver. It was that which was bothering her most. But she still had one hope left. One she hadn't yet mentioned to Nick or even to Detective Chief Inspector Pitcher.

Though Nick had completed his evidence and could have been released from further attendance with the approval of the court, Pitcher had told him that he ought to be around when the hearing resumed the next morning.

As he and Clare entered the court building, Pitcher detached himself from the small group of people to whom he'd been talking and came across. Clare noticed that one of them was Detective Chief Superintendent Upperton who gave Nick a quick glance and then turned away.

Pitcher had the air of someone who'd been up most of the night. His eyes looked as clear as half-chewed wine gums.

"The prosecution's going to ask for an adjournment," he said, looking at Clare. When she didn't reply, he went on, "Don't you want to know why, Mrs. Attwell?"

"Why?"

"Because I've found the piece of paper. Also because I've traced the window cleaner. As you can probably tell I've had quite a busy night."

"You mean, sir, that my wife's guesswork proved correct?"

"I mean, Nick, that if she were still in the force, she'd be either thrown out or instantly promoted. I'm not sure which. Though I know what my recommendation would be." He gave them a tired grin. "Anyway, we're seeking a week's adjournment on the grounds of further enquiries which will now be necessary." He paused. "It's too soon to say how all this is going to affect you, Nick. Naturally, I've told Mr. Upperton the position."

As they entered the courtroom, Nick and Clare separated. Clare was pleased to see that Alice Macpherson had turned up again and she squeezed in next to her. Looking round, she noticed Paul Frensham in earnest conversation with his father and lawyers. For once, he appeared to be taking a lively interest in what was going on.

Over on the far side, she saw Oliver Gill talking to Mrs. Rawlings who was staring straight ahead of her with her customary air of strong disapproval. Once or twice she gave a stiff nod, but this was the extent of her engagement in the conversation.

A few minutes later everyone rose as Mrs. Dowell and her fellow magistrates took their places on the bench. As soon as everyone had sat down again, Mr. Jude came to his feet.

"When we adjourned yesterday afternoon, madam, I was anticipating calling the remainder of my witnesses this morning and concluding the evidence for the prosecution. However, there has been an unforeseen development overnight which obliges me to ask for an adjournment. I cannot, I'm afraid, be more specific other than to say that the development to which I refer will require the police to make certain enquiries. What their ultimate effect on this case will be, I cannot foretell, but it is clearly, in my submission, in the interests of both prosecution and defence that the case now be adjourned."

The clerk glanced frostily at Mr. Croxley. "Do you wish to add anything?"

"Most certainly I do," Mr. Croxley retorted in an imperious tone. Focusing a stern gaze on the magistrates, he went on, "This is not only a most unusual application, but one made, moreover, on the flimsiest of grounds. Indeed, we're not even vouchsafed the knowledge of those grounds. Further enquiries! What further enquiries I pray? My learned friend has the temerity to tell you that these mysterious further enquiries are to be made in the interests of both the prosecution and the defence. Well, he speaks for himself! The defence say that you should refuse this application. We are quite willing to run the risks involved in the hearing continuing today, because we don't accept that there are any risks. In due course, I shall be confidently submitting to you that my client has no case to answer. It is a submission I wish to make at the earliest moment and I strenuously oppose this application for an adjournment."

The clerk stood up and turning his back on the court held a short whispered colloquy with the three magistrates.

He had no sooner resumed his seat than Mrs. Dowell announced, "We will adjourn the case for three days."

At once the courtroom became a parrot-house of chatter as people pushed toward the exits.

"What was all that in aid of?" Gill asked, coming up to Pitcher in the lobby.

"I thought you might have guessed, Mr. Gill. Anyway, I'm glad I caught you before you left. We'll go over to my office."

"What is this?" Gill's tone betrayed a note of worry.

"It's about a piece of paper and a window cleaner. Though we'll talk about them in the reverse order."

Chapter 24

"What's all this nonsense about a window cleaner?" Gill asked crossly when they were seated in Pitcher's office with Sergeant Lyle also present. "I don't know what you're talking about. What window cleaner?"

"You mentioned him when you were giving evidence yesterday. Remember?"

"I remember my evidence very clearly and it had nothing to do with a window cleaner. It was confined to my aunt's identification."

For a few seconds, Pitcher didn't speak, but continued staring at Gill as if sizing up an opponent in the ring.

"It was in answer to a question in cross-examination," he said quietly. "Mr. Croxley was asking you about your aunt's disposition and you were agreeing that she was a difficult person." He paused. "Remember?"

"I think so," Gill said with a petulant frown. "I hope I'm not expected to remember every question I was asked by that old windbag!"

"You volunteered the information that the last time you visited your aunt she complained about the new window cleaner she'd engaged. He should have turned up that day but hadn't."

"If you say so."

"It was *you* who said so, Mr. Gill."

"And what if I did?"

"You'd earlier told the court that the last occasion you visited your aunt was about a week before her death."

"That's right."

"But the day on which the new window cleaner was due to come was the day of her death."

"What are you suggesting?" Gill's tone was an angry bluster.

"That you visited your aunt on the day of her death."

"What nonsense!"

"You see, we've traced the window cleaner. His name's Stanley Pilling. Your aunt had only got in touch with him the day before her death and he'd promised to call and do the windows the next day. But then he found he was overbooked and he gave preference to his regular customers and your aunt's windows went dirty. And that's what she complained to you about. And that's what you told the court yesterday." Gill sat very still, gripping the sides of his chair. "What's more," Pitcher went on, "as soon as you'd volunteered that, you realised what a ghastly mistake you'd made. Your expression gave you away. There were people in court who noticed it and began to wonder what was the explanation."

Pitcher thought it was likely that others in addition to Clare had observed his sudden change of demeanour, but that only she had drawn the right conclusion.

"You'll be suggesting next that I killed my aunt," Gill said with a small scornful smile.

"Did you?"

"It doesn't say very much for the police when you've already charged someone else."

"That hasn't answered my question."

"Of course, I didn't kill her. She mayn't have been my favorite person, but I certainly had no motive for murdering her. You might be on stronger grounds with your insinuations if I'd stood to benefit under her will."

"Or if you weren't really her nephew?"

Gill looked as though he'd received a hard blow to the head. His jaw sagged and he blinked stupidly.

"That was your motive, wasn't it?" Pitcher went on. "You'd just learnt that you weren't her nephew at all. You were her son."

For several seconds Gill tried to speak, but no words came.

169

"Get him some water," Pitcher said and Lyle left the room. When he returned, Gill took the glass from him and drank the contents in noisy gulps.

"Her *illegitimate* son at that," he said in a choked voice. "Adopted and brought up by an uncle and aunt whom I'd always believed to be my true parents." He went on bitterly, "And not even when they were killed by a flying bomb and I was only four years old did my real mother look after me. I was farmed out to foster parents, while she remained remote in *her* adopted role of aunt."

"And you only discovered the truth just before her death?"

Gill nodded painfully. "She told me that afternoon and I just lost all control. I killed her on a sudden impulse. My mind was temporarily unbalanced."

"I don't think it happened quite like that," Pitcher said quietly.

"What do you mean?"

"What happened was that Unsworth found a letter from your supposed mother to the deceased which made it clear whose son you were. The deceased discovered what he'd done. Either he taxed her with it or she caught him in the act, it doesn't really matter which. The upshot was they had a first class row and Unsworth was told to pack his bags and go. My guess is that, in a mood of spite, he got in touch with you and told you the truth. And it was armed with that knowledge you went to the house and killed the woman you'd always believed to be your aunt.

"My further guess is that Unsworth never really believed the murder had been committed by Frensham. It was too much of a coincidence that Mrs. Isaacs was found murdered so soon after he'd told you what he'd found out. We know that he returned to the house after the murder to look for the letter. Instead, he was knocked on the head by a young burglar named Rivings and he left empty-handed. But he went to the house because he realised that if he could find the letter again, it might be turned to profit. But even when he didn't find it, he saw no reason not to let you think he had it in his possession."

Gill's eyes had become hypnotically fixed on Pitcher's face. "In short, Unsworth was a blackmailer and like so many of that ilk he came to a sticky end. Or in his case, a watery one." He paused. "I'm expecting to prove that he was assisted into the river by a clout on the back of the head. Shall I be right?"

Gill said nothing, but sat slumped in a daze.

"Last night," Pitcher continued, "I made a personal search of your aunt's . . . your mother's house and I found the letter we've been talking about." He reached into a drawer. "Here's a photostat if you'd like to read it." He passed the sheet of shiny paper across to Gill who took it in his fingers and stared at it with unseeing eyes. "Let me read it to you then," Pitcher said, taking another copy from the drawer. "It's dated 14th August 1944 and reads as follows: 'Dear Florence, Yesterday was little Oliver's fourth birthday and such a happy one. He is, I'm sure, going to grow up to be the son Leonard and I always longed for but were unable to have. I know you don't like being reminded of his fatherless birth but now that your own Frank is dead I hope you may feel able to rejoice in him as a 'nephew' in a way you were unable to accept him as a son. Your affectionate sister, Dorothea.' "

"Two months later she and Leonard were dead," Gill said dully.

"Have you any idea who was your real father?"

He shook his head. "It was soon after the outbreak of war. Uncle Frank had been called up. My . . . my mother met some man. I was the result. She tried to have an abortion. In the end she had me at . . . . at Aunt Dorothea's. As soon as she was fit enough, she just walked out of the house and left me there."

"Did she tell you this herself?"

"She was furious that Unsworth had told me and she hurled it at me like abuse as though I was to blame for everything that had ever gone wrong in her life. I saw then that she really hated me and I picked up that thing and hit her to stop her. Afterwards, I had to hide as Frensham came upstairs. I suppose he must have heard a noise. I slipped out of the house after he'd gone."

He paused breathless and held out the empty glass to be refilled. Pitcher waited until Sergeant Lyle returned with more water.

Then he said, "Shall we now get all this down in a written statement?"

171

Chapter 25

By the time the court reconvened three days later, the D.P.P.'s department had informed Frensham's solicitors that it was not proposed to offer any further evidence against him.

Jude's mandate was to accomplish this as smoothly as possible, though he was only too well aware that nothing he said would prevent Mr. Croxley contributing a strong measure of forensic fire and brimstone.

News of what was impending had spread through the grapevine so that the courtroom was more crowded than ever, with the press, in particular, assembled in full strength. Sir Guy had seen to that all right.

To Clare's dismay, the row in which she had been sitting was filled to overflowing, but Sergeant Lyle rescued her and put her into a seat behind the court inspector.

When she thanked him, he said with a deadpan wink, "Seeing what you've stirred up, you deserve to be here when the brickbats fly."

Glancing about her, she noticed Paul Frensham talking to his father. Although he appeared quite animated, his face still had a hooded, secretive look. Clare decided that his expression was one of complete self-centredness. She wondered if he was capable of any feeling for others, except when it suited him. As she watched, his solicitor came up and joined father and son.

Meanwhile Mr. Croxley was talking to Jude who was listening with an air of detachment as defending counsel clearly rehearsed some of the strictures he'd soon be passing in open court.

On the far side sat Pitcher with Sergeant Lyle next to him on one side and Detective Chief Superintendent Upperton on the other. He looked tired and dispirited and Clare felt a sudden pang of sympathy for him. She hoped that nothing she had done was going to prejudice his career. But as the officer in charge of the case, she realised he couldn't be feeling very happy.

There was a sudden surge to the feet as the magistrates entered. Mrs. Dowell looked at Jude and said, "I believe you have something to say to the court, Mr. Jude?"

"Yes, madam. When we adjourned three days ago, I informed the court that the public interest necessitated further urgent enquiries being made. I said at the time that I was unable to forecast what their effect might be on the course of this hearing." He paused and went on gravely, "As a result of these enquiries another person will shortly be charged with the murder of Mrs. Isaacs and the prosecution is offering no further evidence against this accused and is inviting you to discharge him." He paused again. "Having said that, madam, I wish to add that, in the prosecution's view, no-one on their side is to blame for this accused having been charged and subjected to this hearing. . . ."

"What you're saying, Mr. Jude," the clerk broke in, "is that the accused has only himself to blame for his predicament?"

Jude nodded while Mr. Croxley scribbled in his notebook and did some furious underlining.

"I must be careful, madam, what I say in view of the fact that another person is to be charged with this crime and I am sure you will appreciate that the situation is a delicate one. All I need add is that the prosecution, by which I mean the department I represent as well as the police, have given this matter the most careful consideration and are satisfied beyond doubt that the course which is now being taken is the only proper one in all the circumstances."

Mr. Croxley rose like some outraged deity and glared down at Jude for a moment before starting to address the magistrates.

"I cannot recall in all my experience at the Bar," he said in a tone

173

like stage thunder, "having ever heard such an outrageous speech. The fact is that the prosecution in this case have blundered—yes, blundered—in the most disgraceful way. This in effect they admit. But are they contrite? Do they apologise? Far from it; they shamelessly seek to justify what has happened and to excuse themselves with words as glib as any it has ever been my misfortune to hear in a court of law."

At this point, Mr. Newsome let out a large yawn.

"This young man," Mr. Croxley went on, gesturing dramatically in Paul Frensham's direction, "has had this grave charge hanging over his head for all these weeks. He has at all times protested his innocence and now at the eleventh hour and fifty-ninth minute the prosecution grudgingly recognise that fact. And do so, as I've already remarked, without a breath of apology. My learned friend had the temerity to suggest that my client had only himself to blame for what had happened. Well, your worships, let him and the police be assured that we shall not let the matter rest there. It will be raised with the appropriate authorities at the highest level with a view not merely to obtaining some form of restitution for all the suffering my young client has endured, but to ensuring so far as is possible that no other innocent person can ever be subjected to a similar ordeal."

With his words still ringing in people's ears, Mr. Croxley abruptly sat down.

"Paul Frensham, the charge against you is dismissed," Mrs. Dowell announced quickly and at once retired with her fellow magistrates from the bench.

Sir Guy Frensham stood with a protective arm round his son's shoulders as newspapermen milled about them.

"No press conference in court please," the court inspector called out loudly.

Clare waited in her seat until the crowd had thinned. As she reached the exit, she found herself immediately behind the Frenshams who were still being besieged by reporters.

"Can you say whether your son's complaint against Sergeant Attwell still stands, Sir Guy?" she heard one of them ask.

Sir Guy Frensham paused and turned his head toward the questioner.

"It not only stands," he said loudly, "but I shall now be pressing the Commissioner for prompt action against the officer."

Chapter 26

Simon seemed surprised but not displeased to have both his parents back in time for lunch—and celebrated the event by spooning his food on to the floor where it fell with such a fascinating plop that he was encouraged to attempt a repeat performance.

It was while Clare was cleaning up the mess that the phone rang and Nick went to answer it.

"It's Alice Macpherson for you," he said, returning to the kitchen a few seconds later.

"I wonder what she wants," Clare remarked as she went to take the call.

"Hello, Clare," Alice sounded a trifle breathless. "I'd hoped you'd answer. I thought Nick sounded a bit put out when I asked to speak to you."

"He hasn't got used to our knowing each other, that's all. We only got back from court half an hour ago."

"I'm sorry I wasn't there but I couldn't get away this morning. What I wanted to let you know, Clare, is that Betsy had a letter from Kersty today. She's read it to me over the phone. Kersty's decided not to come back to London. She said things had become too complicated and she didn't want to get further mixed up in them. She mentioned that she had a friend working in a hotel in California and was thinking of joining her if she could scrape together the money for the fare." Alice paused. "And that was really all. She did add that she hadn't liked letting down the British police who'd treated her decently, but that she was more afraid of Sir Guy Frensham than of them. It sounds as if she's putting the past behind her, Clare."

"I see," Clare said bleakly.

"Perhaps she hadn't received your letter when she wrote to Betsy," Alice remarked in a hopeful tone.

"Even if she had, I don't suppose Nick's fate means anything to her. After all, she'd never even met him."

"Don't give up hope yet. And if there's anything else I can do, give me a call. I must dash now, Clare, I have to feed the kids."

Nick looked up expectantly as Clare returned to the kitchen.

"What did Alice want?" he asked.

"She only phoned to say that Betsy had had a letter from Kerstin Borg and that she's decided not to come back to England. She's going to California."

"So?"

"That's all."

Clare had no heart to tell Nick how she had sent a letter to Kersty asking her to write to the British police and inform them that Paul Frensham's accusation was false, if she knew it to be so.

"I can see every reason for her not coming back," Nick said dispassionately. "I don't imagine the Frenshams are too anxious to have her back in this country after all that's happened." He gazed for a moment at Simon who was conducting an imaginary band with his spoon. "Shall I tell you what's going to happen? Upperton will in due course report that it's a question of word against word and that Frensham's allegation is accordingly non-proven, as there's no independent evidence to show where the truth lies. The evidence against me being insufficient to justify either criminal or disciplinary proceedings, I shall be instructed to return to duty. But because Sir Guy Frensham will make one hell of a public song and dance about rooting out corruption in the police and protecting innocent boys from depraved officers, I shall be quietly transferred to the most distant neck of the woods they can find, where they'll hope I grow moss and merge into the background."

He paused and went on in a tone of utter dejection. "That's what's going to happen, but it's not a fate I'm prepared to accept. They can have my job rather than that." He noticed Clare's anxious expression. "I mean it. I didn't join the police to be shunted into a limbo kept for tainted officers."

"I know how you feel, darling, but it's too soon for such talk." Clare came across and stood behind his chair, lacing her hands round his neck. "I'm sure Upperton's on your side. The odds are he'll now be able to get Paul Frensham to admit his allegation was false."

Nick shook his head. "That's not realistic, Clare, and you know it. Frensham realises that if he does that he'll be prosecuted for making a false report and wasting police time. He's stuck with his allegation whether he wants to be or not." In a tone full of bitterness, he added, "And he wants to be, all right."

Clare bent and kissed the top of her husband's head, at which point Simon who had become bored gave his chair a sudden tilt backwards and banged his head against the wall.

"Serves you right," Nick remarked as he rescued his son and set about comforting him.

Later in the afternoon, Nick and Simon accompanied Clare when she went out shopping. They returned shortly after four o'clock and hadn't been in the house more than a few minutes before the telephone began ringing.

"You go," Nick said. "It's probably Alice again."

"I doubt it," Clare replied. A moment later she returned to the room. "It's Detective Sergeant Young and he wants to speak to you."

Nick wasn't away for more than a couple of minutes and when he came back he wore a puzzled expression.

"The professor's on his way here. Young was only ringing to make sure we were in."

"We?"

"Yes. Apparently he'd like to see both of us."

While they awaited Upperton's arrival, Nick paced restlessly from room to room, leaving Clare to keep Simon amused. When the bell rang, Nick rushed to open the front door.

"Good evening, Mrs. Attwell," Upperton said as he came into the living-room. "And hello to you, sir," he added gravely to Simon who stared at him in silent wonder. Sitting down, he turned to Clare and said, "I gather you've been in touch with Miss Borg in Sweden?"

"Yes, I wrote to her."

Upperton nodded. "It's not clear whether she's responding to your letter or to her own conscience. Perhaps a bit of both. At all events she called at the British Embassy in Stockholm this morning and said that she wished to make a statement in the presence of a consular official. I've not yet seen the statement and it'll be coming over in the diplomatic bag, but we've received a telexed version via the Foreign Office. Briefly, she confirms what I personally had always believed, namely that Frensham made his allegation against you in order to discredit you. He was sure you'd spotted her red earring in his bedroom and sooner or later would connect it with the green one which had dropped off his sweater when he went up to Mrs. Isaacs' bedroom. He'd apparently been in the house looking for cash which, as we've heard, the old lady was apt to leave around, when he heard groans coming from upstairs and went to investigate. She seems to have died while he was actually bending over her and he fled in panic. On his return from the police station he told Kersty what had happened—though I gather he never told his father the whole story—and she was greatly concerned that it was *her* earring which had become mislaid. Of course, it wasn't until later that he actually knew he'd dropped it in the bedroom, though he seems to have thought it likely. Hence his allegation against you, Sergeant."

Nick let out a long sigh and reached for Clare's hand.

"As soon as I receive the statement," Upperton went on, "I'll be able to complete my report. It will, of course, have to be submitted to the D.P.P. for decision, but I anticipate its arrival will have two swift results. Your reinstatement and the effective silencing of Sir Guy Frensham."

After the two officers from A.10 had departed, Nick and Clare fell into each other's arms in a long embrace while Simon watched them with growing impatience. Eventually he let out a frustrated bellow.

"O.K., you can join in, too," Nick said, picking him up and planting a kiss on his cheek.

"I'll take him up to bed," Clare said later when Simon's evening romp was over. "I think you ought to make a phone call while I'm upstairs."

Nick looked mystified for a moment. "Oh, you mean to Alice?" Clare nodded. "Yes, I'll call her and tell her what's happened," Nick said, immediately.

Later, as he waited for her phone to be answered, he fell to reflecting how different the course of events might have been had some unknown thief not stolen her purse in the Abbey that afternoon. But for that, they would never have met and if they'd never met . . . .

"Is that you, Alice? It's Nick Attwell. I've just had wonderful news."

THE END

>>> If you've enjoyed this book and would like to discover more great vintage crime and thriller titles, as well as the most exciting crime and thriller authors writing today, visit: >>>

The Murder Room
Where Criminal Minds Meet

themurderroom.com